SPECIAL MESSAGE TO READERS

THE ULVERSCROFT FOUNDATION (registered UK charity number 264873) was established in 1972 to provide funds for research, diagnosis and treatment of eye diseases. Examples of major projects funded by the Ulverscroft Foundation are:—

- The Children's Eye Unit at Moorfields Eye Hospital, London
- The Ulverscroft Children's Eye Unit at Great Ormond Street Hospital for Sick Children
- Funding research into eye diseases and treatment at the Department of Ophthalmology, University of Leicester
- The Ulverscroft Vision Research Group, Institute of Child Health
- Twin operating theatres at the Western Ophthalmic Hospital, London
- The Chair of Ophthalmology at the Royal Australian College of Ophthalmologists

You can help further the work of the Foundation by making a donation or leaving a legacy. Every contribution is gratefully received. If you would like to help support the Foundation or require further information, please contact:

THE ULVERSCROFT FOUNDATION
The Green, Bradgate Road, Anstey
Leicester LE7 7FU, England
Tel: (0116) 236 4325

website: www.foundation.ulverscroft.com

SPECIAL MESSAGE TO READERS

THE ULVERSCROFT FOUNDATION
(registered UK charity number 264873)
was established in 1972 to provide funds for research, diagnosis and treatment of eye diseases. Examples of major projects funded by the Ulverscroft Foundation are:-

- The Children's Eye Unit at Moorfields Eye Hospital, London
- The Ulverscroft Children's Eye Unit at Great Ormond Street Hospital for Sick Children
- Funding research into eye diseases and treatment at the Department of Ophthalmology, University of Leicester
- The Ulverscroft Vision Research Group, Institute of Child Health
- Twin operating theatres at the Western Ophthalmic Hospital, London
- The Chair of Ophthalmology at the Royal Australian College of Ophthalmologists

You can help further the work of the Foundation by making a donation or leaving a legacy. Every contribution is gratefully received. If you would like to help support the Foundation or require further information, please contact:

THE ULVERSCROFT FOUNDATION
The Green, Bradgate Road, Anstey
Leicester LE7 7FU, England
Tel: (0116) 236 4325

website: www.foundation.ulverscroft.com

STORM CHASER

When Caitlin Mulryan graduates from university and returns to Stargate, the small Dorset village where she grew up, she is dismayed to find that the longstanding feud between her family and the Kingtons is as fierce as ever. Soon her twin brother is hunted down in his boat *Storm Chaser* by his bitter enemy, with tragedy in their wake — and Caitlin can only blame herself for her foolish actions. So falling in love with handsome Yorkshireman Nick Thorne is the last thing on her mind . . .

Books by Paula Williams
in the Linford Romance Library:

PLACE OF HEALING
FINDING ANNABEL
MOUNTAIN SHADOWS

PAULA WILLIAMS

STORM CHASER

Complete and Unabridged

LINFORD
Leicester

First published in Great Britain in 2015

First Linford Edition
published 2016

A catalogue record for this book is available from the British Library.

ISBN 978–1–4448–2841–2

Published by
F. A. Thorpe (Publishing)
Anstey, Leicestershire

Set by Words & Graphics Ltd.
Anstey, Leicestershire
Printed and bound in Great Britain by
T. J. International Ltd., Padstow, Cornwall

This book is printed on acid-free paper

1

Everything is relative. Even bad news. And the day before my graduation from uni, I reckoned I'd had the bad news day to end all bad news days.

It was the culmination of three years of hard work and should have been up there with one of the best of them. Instead it started badly and got progressively worse. By the time I crawled into bed that night, I honestly believed I'd had the Day From Hell, the worst day of my life.

Looking back on it now, of course, I can see I was wrong. There were far, far worse days to come. But that's hindsight for you, isn't it?

My Day From Hell began with Matt, shuffling his feet and refusing to look me in the eye as he said: 'It's not you, Caitlin. It's me.'

How corny is that? Eight months into

our on/off relationship and he couldn't come up with a more original line than that? Of course it was him. He was the one telling me that he was off grape-picking in France instead of coming down to Dorset with me as we'd planned. That he needed 'some space, to sort my head out'. Like his head was one gigantic, messed-up jigsaw puzzle.

What he didn't tell me, although I found out later that day when I overheard a couple of girls talking about it in the ladies', was that he was going off to sort his head out with a bottle-blonde second-year student with giraffe-like eyelashes and legs up to her armpits, whose daddy just happened to own said vineyard in France.

'Not that there will be much grape-picking going on. From what I heard, they can't keep their hands off each other,' one of them sniggered and they both collapsed in giggles — until they saw me standing behind them, glaring at them in the hazed mirror.

It was the pity in their eyes that got me. I can't say I was heartbroken about Matt. Whatever there had been between us had run its course and, to be honest, it might as easily have been me doing the 'it's not you, it's me' line, although I like to think I'd have come up with something more original. But those pitying looks? They really rankled.

So when my phone rang a few minutes later and I saw it was Dad calling, my grumpy mood got a whole heap grumpier. Dad never called me during the day. Unless . . .

'Yes, Dad, what is it?'

'Caitlin. Listen, sweetheart. I'm very sorry. Bad news, I'm afraid.'

My heart sank like a punctured balloon. As I said, he never called me during the day, and hardly ever called me sweetheart. It had to be bad if he was doing both. And I'd a pretty good idea what form that bad news was going to take.

I stepped into the entrance of a nearby coffee shop as the first fat splats of rain dotted the pavement. 'Let me guess. You're not coming tomorrow,' I said, making no attempt to hide my disappointment.

'Well, no. Sadly not. The thing is, you see, I've a very important appointment that I just cannot get out of, and — '

'So have I, Dad,' I snapped at the same time as I glared at some unfortunate man who was trying to squeeze by me. I moderated my voice to an angry hiss. 'It's called a graduation ceremony and you agreed to be there, remember?'

I wanted to run after the man and apologise, tell him I didn't make a habit of being rude; it was just that my father was the most infuriating man on the planet.

'Sure I remember, sweetheart,' Dad was saying. 'And it's breaking my heart that I can't be with you on such an important occasion, so it is.' Although it was nearly thirty years since Dad had lived in his native Ireland, his accent always became thicker when he was under stress. At that moment, he sounded more like an advert for the Visit Ireland tourist campaign than my father.

'Don't worry about it,' I said, my voice as chilly as the rain now bouncing off the pavement. 'I'll be fine.'

'Well, now, look. Maggie's offered to come in my place. How would that do?'

'No. That would not do at all,' I said firmly. I'd already been subjected to pitying looks once today. I hated the thought of Maggie, who disliked travelling at the best of times, dragging herself all the way down to Exeter because she, too, felt sorry for me. 'Tell Maggie thank you for the offer, but I'm fine. There will be loads of people there on their own. It's no big deal.'

'Look, about getting home — Liam has said he'll pick you up from Dorchester station if you can get the train.'

'Fine. I'll text him with the time of the train,' I said. Then I told him some pathetic lie about having to dash off to an end-of-year party and rang off.

I pushed open the door to the coffee shop, thinking of treating myself to a hot chocolate with extra marshmallows, but the man I'd glared at was in the queue ahead of me and gave me such a frightened look that I left and sloshed through the rain back to my room. I spent the rest of the day moping around, feeling sorry for myself and kicking myself for having refused Maggie's kind offer.

And my point about everything being relative, even bad news? I remember thinking as I finally drifted off to sleep that night that my Day From Hell had been one of the worst days of my life.

How very, very wrong I was.

2

'What do you mean, you can't make it?' I yelled, even though I hate it when people shout into their mobiles loud enough for everyone within a five-mile radius to hear. But my brother Liam wasn't within a five-mile radius — and that was the problem. I was at Dorchester Station and he was nowhere to be seen. 'What am I supposed to do now? Walk the fifteen miles to Stargate?'

'No, of course not. But couldn't you get a taxi?'

My credit card was maxed out, my student loan exhausted weeks ago; and having to buy a train ticket at the last minute from Exeter to Dorchester had taken the last of my dwindling cash.

'I haven't got enough money for the bus fare, you idiot, let alone a taxi. Besides, I've got a mountain of stuff.' A mountain that was in imminent danger of erupting all over the station concourse as I struggled to hang on to a bulging rucksack and three full-to-bursting carrier bags.

'Go and grab yourself a coffee or something. I'll be there as soon as I can.'

Yesterday my dad, today my brother. What was it about the men in my family that they couldn't turn up when they said they were going to? I still hadn't forgiven Dad for pulling out of my graduation ceremony yesterday. And now Liam, who'd promised faithfully to meet me off the train, was nowhere to be seen. Hence the phone call.

'Hang on a moment. I've got to put this down.' I shuffled around like an incompetent juggler as the handle of the heaviest, most overstuffed carrier bag began to stretch ominously. 'So where are you now, Liam? And how long are you going to be?'

'I'm on my way to Poole. I'll be in Dorchester by five at the latest, I promise. Oh, and Cait?'

'What?'

'You won't tell Dad, will you?'

'That you left me stranded at Dorchester station? You bet your life I will.'

'No, I mean about me going to Poole. The thing is, he doesn't know, and it's a bit . . . '

'Complicated?' I finished the sentence for him, as I often did. Liam was my twin and people thought it was a twin thing. But it wasn't. With Liam, things were often complicated and most of the time, he was the one creating the complication. Like now.

'Cheers. I knew you'd be cool,' he said. 'Catch you later.'

He rang off before I could tell him that I was anything but cool. Instead I fished in my bag for my purse and tried to work out whether I had enough money for that extra-large hot chocolate with all the toppings that I'd passed up on yesterday. In my present mood, coffee just wasn't going to cut it.

'Excuse me.' The deep male voice

behind me made me jump.

'Sorry,' I muttered, although the tone of voice suggested I was anything but as I knelt down and began the near hopeless task of moving my carrier-bag mountain out of his way. Would it have hurt him to have walked around me? I know I was taking up quite a lot of space, but by the time I'd grabbed one bag I'd dropped the other two, and was now causing a serious obstruction.

'Here, let me,' he said. 'I wasn't asking you to move. Only if I could help.'

If that wasn't the story of my life. There I was, red of face and wild of hair, looking like some mad old bag lady with everything I owned scattered around me like the leftovers from a car boot sale. And there he was: smoky blue-grey eyes; slightly-too-long dark hair; and a voice, with its hint of a north-country accent, that made me think for the second time in as many minutes of warm, dark chocolate. That was the good bit.

The bad bit was that he was holding the bag that contained my dirty washing — smelly socks, greying underwear, the lot. The bag with the stretchy handle that was threatening to fall apart at any moment.

'Thanks,' I muttered. 'It's OK. I'll take it.'

He ignored my outstretched hand and picked up another bag. 'Look, I couldn't help overhearing you mention a place called Stargate. Would that be Stargate Bay? Because that's where I'm headed. Would you like a lift?'

Aunt Bridget, my Dad's older sister who had looked after me and Liam for a while after Mum died, taught us not to accept lifts from strangers. On the other hand, she also taught me to use my initiative and not hang around outside wind-blown train stations causing an obstruction while waiting for a waste-of-space brother who might or might not turn up any time before midnight.

'That would be brilliant, thanks.' I smiled gratefully and followed him towards the car park, fighting the urge to snatch my washing back. I almost had to break out into a run to keep up with his long stride.

'Are you down here on holiday?' I asked when I finally caught up with him, and once my carrier-bag mountain was stowed safely in the boot of his rugged black four-by-four that looked as if it should be herding stray cattle across North American plains rather than weaving its way through Dorchester's congested streets.

'No. I'm working here.'

Aunt Bridget had also taught me it was rude to ask direct questions. Then again, she'd said the leprechauns would bite my toes off if I didn't wear my wellington boots in the rain. So I'd long ago learned to be selective when it came to taking her advice.

'Doing what?' I asked directly.

'I'm a building project manager,' he said as he threaded the big car through the traffic and out on to the always-manic A35 with practised ease.

'A building project? In Stargate?'

I was born and bred in Stargate Bay and, much as I love the place, believe me, it isn't as pretty as it sounds. You don't find pictures of it on postcards extolling the beauties of Dorset's Jurassic Coast or hordes of tourists blocking the lanes on a bank holiday. In fact, Stargate Bay itself (as opposed to the village of Higher Stargate half a mile further up the hill) is nothing more than a scruffy, pebbly beach and a pub, set well back from the beach, called The Sailor's Return, that looks like it gave up waiting for the sailor, or anyone else, decades ago. Then there's Sam's little grey 1930s bungalow that was now almost engulfed by his out-of-control garden since his wife died, and a ramshackle tearoom that only opens when Maggie, the owner, feels like it. Which isn't often.

Then, of course, there's my dad's house right at the far end. The oldest building in Stargate Bay, it was built for functionality rather than prettiness. With stone walls two feet thick and tiny windows, and bleached by centuries of wind and sun, it hunkered down under a slate roof ready to withstand whatever the tides and weather threw at it. Next to it was the boathouse and yard and the stone jetty that we think was probably built the same time as the house.

So where, I wondered, was this building project going to be? It was on the tip of my tongue to make a joke about whether old Sam next door had finally decided to have a new porch built on the front of his bungalow (he'd been promising to do it for as long as I'd known him) when I remembered Liam saying how our local Mr Big, a property developer called Andrew Kington, had taken on a new guy from 'up north', which in our part of Dorset can mean anywhere from Bristol upwards.

'Oh, wow. Look at that.' My heart lifted as the busy road crested the top of a hill and the stunning coastline (the bit that does make it onto the postcards) was laid out in front of us like a glorious Technicolor relief map. Deep wooded valleys and rolling hills were fringed with golden cliffs that led down to a turquoise sea. 'I've been travelling this road all my life, in all winds and weathers, and that view still takes my breath away. Every single time.'

'I know what you mean. It's pretty amazing, isn't it?' he said; then spoilt it by adding, 'For the soft south.'

I liked the way his eyes crinkled when he grinned so I let him get away with it. I leaned back in the soft leather seat and settled down to enjoy the ride and to winkle as much information out of him as I could, particularly if it involved Andrew Kington. Anything he was up to was of immense interest to Dad.

'So, tell me to mind my own business if you like, but do you work for Andrew Kington, by any chance?'

'Mind your own business,' he said, with another eye-crinkling grin that robbed his words of any offence. He laughed and added, 'Well, come on. You asked for that.'

'Fair enough,' I said. 'But, tell me, what on earth is Andrew Kington doing employing a project manager in Stargate, of all places?'

'How do you know I'm working for him?'

'You're a project manager with a north-country accent. Andrew Kington has just taken on a new man from up north and is the only guy in the area likely to employ a project manager. I'm right, aren't I?'

'Guilty as charged,' he said with a grin as we slowed down for the ever-present traffic queues at the approach to the busy market town of Bridport.

'So what project are you going to manage?' I was reluctant to let the matter drop.

'It's all at a very early planning stage,' he said vaguely. 'And like so many things, it probably won't even get off the ground. Do you know Stargate well?'

'I should do. I was born and bred there, although I've been away at uni in Exeter for the last three years. My Dad, Joe, owns the little boatyard down the far end. I'm Caitlin Mulryan.'

'Nick Thorne.'

I smiled across at him. 'I really appreciate the lift, Nick. Knowing my brother, I'd have been kicking my heels in Dorchester until midnight.'

'Glad to have helped,' he said. 'You could always repay me by coming out for a drink and a bite to eat one evening soon. I'm still finding my way around but I hear there are some great eating places in the area.'

I'd have been tempted if it wasn't for the fact that I was off men forever, thanks to the pathetic 'it's not you, it's me' rat whose name I've erased from my memory, along with the humiliation of the way he dumped me and the leggy, giraffe-eyed blonde he'd dumped me for. But it was good for my still-bruised ego to be asked. Particularly by a man with — did I mention?

— smoky grey-blue eyes and a voice like warm chocolate.

So I was surprised to hear myself answer, 'That would be good.' And even more surprised to find I meant it.

'Great. I suppose you're busy tonight? First night home, and all that.'

'Yeah. Family stuff. Killing the fatted calf, or whatever's on three for the price of two at Morrisons. But Liam and I will probably be in the Sailor's early for a quick drink before dinner. You're welcome to join us and tell my brother what a lowlife he is for leaving me stranded like he did. He can buy you that drink he owes you.'

'I might well take you up on that.'

As he eased the large vehicle along the narrow lane that led down into Stargate, I couldn't help thinking that a lift home and a possible date, all from accepting a lift from a stranger, suggested to me that it wasn't just the leprechauns Aunt Bridget had been wrong about.

3

Local legend has it that Stargate's pub, The Sailor's Return, was originally the haunt of smugglers. It was built around the same time as our house and had the same huddled look that made it look more like a grey speckled broody hen with its tiny windows, thick walls and low squat roof.

For as long as I can remember it had been run by Jed Martin, who was the only publican I know who regarded customers as a nuisance — they got in the way of his fishing — and did everything he could to discourage them, including refusing to turn on the heating until November 20th, whatever the outside temperature; and whose idea of good pub food was a pickled egg served in a packet of barbecue-flavoured crisps for what he called 'a touch of the exoticals'.

Earlier in the summer, he'd surprised everyone by announcing he was selling up and going to live in Milton Keynes with someone he'd met on the internet. Two weeks later, the pub had been sold in what Dad described as Andrew Kington's latest land grab.

'You wait,' Dad had predicted with gloomy relish. 'He'll turn the place into one of those trendy gastropubs that charge the earth for one lettuce leaf and half an olive and fill it with a load of Hooray Henrys with more money than sense.'

I thought a few Hooray Henrys might liven the place up a bit and could even bring more business to the boatyard, but Dad has always had a blind spot where Andrew Kington is concerned, and refused to believe that the outcome would be anything other than disastrous for Stargate.

As we rounded the final sharp bend, my heart did a leap for joy at the sight of Ben Kington standing in the pub car park with his father Andrew.

I'd been in love with Ben since I fell off my bike in front of him when I was eight and a half years old and he helped me up and straightened my handlebars for me. Sadly for me, though, my puppy-like adoration was strictly a one-way thing. He was a couple of years older than Liam and me. Tall, loose-limbed and blond, with deep blue eyes that made you think of a summer sky. Forget pop idols and sporting heroes — none of them came close to Ben for me. Especially not he-who-shall-not-be-named, who'd put me off men forever. Because, of course, when I said I was off men, that didn't include Ben. He was, and always would be, the exception to every rule in my book.

When we were kids, he could swim the furthest, run the fastest, do the fanciest tricks on his top-of-the-range skateboard. As he got older, that changed to him having the sportiest car, the fastest boat, the coolest clothes. And a smile that could melt the polar ice caps and reduced me to a quivering wreck if he deigned to turn it in my direction. Which, apart from the falling-off-the-bike incident, didn't happen very often. I adored him, even though he didn't even know I existed, except maybe as Liam Mulryan's geeky, painfully shy sister who became tongue-tied in his presence and blushed to the roots of her wild black hair at the sight of him.

He was also Liam's sworn enemy and bitterest rival. And his name and that of his father could not be mentioned in the Mulryan household without my brother and father going ballistic. Which Marci, my roommate from uni who did psychology, insisted merely added to his attraction as far as I was concerned. 'Forbidden fruit' was how she explained it to my layman's mind.

Forbidden fruit he may have been, but he could be one of my five-a-day any time he chose. The sight of him always made me feel like the sun had come out, even on the rainiest day.

'You can drop me here,' I said as

Nick slowed down near the gravel-strewn waste ground that passed for the pub car park. 'I'll walk the rest of the way. It's only round the corner. And thanks for the lift. That was great.'

Andrew and Ben had been deep in conversation — that is, Andrew had been doing all the talking and Ben all the scowling — but they both looked up as the car drove up. Nick pulled in next to a sleek silver open-top sports car that had to be Ben's latest boy toy.

'Nick. You made the early train then. So how did it go?' Andrew Kington began, but stopped in surprise as he saw me climb out of the car. 'Caitlin. I didn't know you were due home yet. It's good to see you.'

'Nick found me stranded at Dorchester Station. And very kindly gave me a lift,' I said, carefully avoiding looking at Ben, as always, although I was acutely aware of his presence. I hurried round to the back of the car, determined that this time I'd get to the bag of dirty washing before Nick did. The thought of it spilling its contents all over Dorchester Station was one thing. But in front of Ben Kington, it simply didn't bear thinking about. 'I can manage, cheers. Thanks again for the lift, Nick. And don't forget about that drink, if you're around later this evening.'

'You're on,' he said.

'So, Caitlin, have you finished at uni?' Andrew asked as I struggled to contain the carrier-bag mountain. 'I heard you did very well.' He turned to Nick. 'This young lady is quite the celebrity of Stargate, you know. She got a first. In maths, of all subjects. Unlike some people around here who, in spite of a very expensive education, didn't even manage a GCSE in maths.'

'Congratulations,' Nick said, while behind him Ben scowled. I gave him a small apologetic smile, which he ignored.

'What's next then?' Andrew went on. 'A highly lucrative job in the City?'

I shook my head. 'Nothing so

glamorous. In the short term I've got a job waitressing in a hotel in Lyme Regis for the summer, and then in September I'm going back to Exeter to do my teacher training.'

Teaching was all I'd ever wanted to do, ever since I was a little girl and used to draw up complicated timetables, spelling tests and reading lists for my toys. Unlike Liam, I'd loved school, particularly maths, and my passion for the subject only increased the higher my level of study. Liam called me seriously weird, while Dad said I must get my aptitude for maths from my mother; it certainly wasn't from him.

'A teacher, eh?' A shadow passed across Andrew's thin face and his voice softened. 'Your mother would have been very proud of you. She always — '

'Well, Dad? Are we going to stand around here all day?' Ben cut in. 'Only, I've promised to meet someone at five. Good to see you back, Caitlin,' he added as an afterthought as he hurried towards his car.

'You go on,' Andrew said. 'I'll get a lift back with Nick. We've got things to discuss.'

As Ben roared up the narrow lane, I pressed my bags tightly to me and walked the short distance to my home, praying all the time that the bags would hold together at least until I was safely round the corner.

* * *

Nick smiled as he and Andrew watched in silence until Caitlin had disappeared around the corner of the pub and turned into the lane that led along the edge of the beach towards the boat house. She was clutching those wretched carrier bags like they were a lifebelt. Poor girl. He'd seen what was in the one that was in imminent danger of breaking and how embarrassed she'd been about it. It was a long time since he'd met a girl who blushed.

Without warning, an image flashed into his mind: Abbie. With her silky blonde hair and blue eyes, she didn't look remotely like this tousle-haired, freckle-faced girl. But there was something about Caitlin — the way she smiled, the way her cheeks flooded scarlet — that reminded him of her. And being reminded of Abbie was the last thing he wanted.

Was that, then, why he'd given in to a spur-of-the-moment thing and asked her out — because something about her reminded him of Abbie? Stupid. Stupid. Stupid. Thank goodness they'd left things vague and not made a firm date.

'So you gave young Caitlin a lift, eh?' Andrew said with a knowing smile. 'Quite the good neighbour, aren't we?'

'She was stranded at Dorchester Station. Her brother was supposed to be picking her up but hadn't turned up.'

A frown flickered across Andrew Kington's hawk-like face. 'That sounds like Liam,' he said. 'You know who she is, don't you?'

'I gathered that she's the daughter of

Joe Mulryan, the owner of the boatyard. The man who stands between you and the marina development.'

'For the moment. The stubborn old fool,' Andrew said. 'The guy's broke, his boatyard's gone belly up; he's just too pig-headed to see it. But I'll have my way eventually. I always do.'

Nick raised an eyebrow. 'Really? He gave me a pretty unequivocal no. Turned the offer down flat, and I'm sure he wasn't holding out for a higher price. If I was you, Mr Kington, I'd start looking at alternative sites.'

'Well, you're not me, are you?' Andrew snapped and there was a coldness in his seal-grey eyes that made Nick realise for the first time that this self-contained, soft-spoken man would make a formidable enemy. 'I will have my marina at Stargate Bay — and no one, least of all Joe Mulryan, is going to stand in my way.'

Nick shrugged. 'Your call,' he said. 'Now, do you want me to take another look at that site? I've had a few thoughts about alternative access.'

Andrew shook his head. 'Not with Caitlin Mulryan hanging about. That's just asking for trouble, and that's something I don't need at the moment.'

'Fair enough.' Nick turned back to the car. 'Are you ready to go then?' he asked, and waited as Andrew climbed in beside him. 'Home or the office?'

'I'm sorry, Nick.' Andrew rubbed a hand over his eyes, lines of weariness etched on his face. 'I didn't mean to snap. Let's head back to the office and you can fill me in on how you got on in London. Then perhaps we could have dinner this evening? There's this lovely fish restaurant in West Bay . . . '

'Thanks. But I have plans.' He didn't, of course. But he was tired and more than a little unsettled. All he wanted was a quick beer somewhere and then the chance to catch up on some paperwork.

'Plans, eh? Would those plans include Caitlin Mulryan by any chance?' Andrew asked.

Nick frowned as he started the car. 'I don't see . . .'

'I'm sorry. I had no right to pry into your private life. It's just that — I thought maybe you could . . .'

'Ask her what her father's plans for the boatyard are? Is that what you're building up to?' Nick said. 'I don't think so.'

'No, of course not. Nothing as crude as that,' Andrew said. 'But on the other hand, if the topic of her father's plans should come up in conversation . . .'

Without meaning to, Andrew had in fact given Nick one more reason to stay away from Caitlin Mulryan. That and the fact that her half-shy, half-defiant way of looking at him from under her lashes took him back to a place where he didn't want to be.

Why, then, had he thought he might, after all, have that quick beer in The Sailor's Return later that evening? Bad, bad idea.

4

The house was deserted, except for the dog who looked up, saw I wasn't Liam (his favourite person on the planet) and settled back to sleep with a deep sigh. 'Hey, come on, Archie, you old lazy bones,' I said. 'Let's go find Dad, shall we?'

A piercing sadness caught me unawares as he got to his feet, the movements in his long, gangly limbs stiff and deliberate. When had he turned into an old dog? It seemed only yesterday Dad had incurred Aunt Bridget's wrath by bringing him home for us. A harum-scarum mess of a dog, he was part Border Collie and part goodness knows what. His whiplash tail should be classified as a lethal weapon while his wiry hair, now greyed around his muzzle, sprouted in every direction, giving him the look of a worn-out bottle brush.

We took the path that led along the edge of the beach to the boat house, where I knew Dad would be. The blue-grey sea was calm today, small wavelets creeping in furtively, almost silently, along the shoreline. The clusters of sea pinks that fringed the edges of the beach had gone over, their candy-floss hue now faded to pale caramel.

Progress was slow as Archie, as always, insisted on stopping to sniff at each individual pebble. But I didn't mind. I was happy to wait, look out across the broad sweep of the bay, and breathe in the tang of salt and seaweed and the scents of home. As I did so, the tension of the last few months — long nights revising for finals, yesterday's graduation, even the 'it's not you, it's me' moment — slipped away. Even my irritation with Liam had faded. I took a long, deep lungful of air 'so fresh you could wash your face in it' (that's Dad's fancy phrase, not mine, by the way). Oh yes, it was good to be home.

Dad looked up from the stripped-down boat engine he was working on as I pushed open the door of the boat house. One look at his face and my good-to-be-home mood vanished.

'Oh, it's yourself,' he grunted. He was still doing his Visit Ireland tourist trailer voice, so obviously his stress levels were still sky-high. 'And where's that brother of yours?'

'I don't know.' At least I was able to answer that truthfully. And I couldn't resist adding in my most sarcastic voice, 'Oh, welcome home, Caitlin. How good to see you.'

He rubbed his oily fingers down his already well-stained overalls, shook his head and sighed. 'I'm sorry. You're quite right to tick me off, sweetheart. It's grand that you're back. Just grand. Only, things are in a bit of a state here. We're run off our feet and I could do with Liam's help. I thought he was meeting you at the station?'

'I got a lift with . . . with a friend,' I

said as the habit of a lifetime took over and I covered up for Liam. Like always.

Anger flared in his eyes. 'For pity's sake, girl, could you not have told us?' He picked up a spanner and went back to his engine, and I couldn't help noticing that we'd gone from 'sweetheart' to 'girl' in a heartbeat. 'We can do without you sending the lad on a wild goose chase to Dorchester and not bothering to tell him you're fixed up.'

'Yes. I can see how busy you are. So much so, you couldn't even make the effort to come to my graduation yesterday,' I snapped as the unfairness of his accusation got all jangled up with the disappointment of his no-show yesterday. I was the only one in my group not to have a fond parent or two clucking around; no proud family group grinning at the photographer. I'd promised myself I'd be all grown up and sensible about it when I saw him. Instead, this stroppy ten-year-old had taken over my head.

'I had . . . things to do,' he mumbled

as he wrestled with a particularly stiff wing nut. 'Things I couldn't get out of.'

'Or wouldn't.' I began to stomp off but he called me back.

'Caitlin. I'm sorry. Truly I am.' He pushed his hands through his hair, leaving an oily smudge across his left temple. 'Your mother would have been that proud, so she would.'

'Unlike you,' the stroppy ten-year-old butted in.

He sighed. 'That's where you're wrong, sweetheart. Come on, let's away into the house and I'll try to explain. And didn't Maggie come along this morning with one of your favourite chocolate cakes as a welcome home present?'

I ditched the stroppy ten-year-old and followed him. But as we reached the kitchen door, I stopped and looked back down the hall. Something was missing. I couldn't believe I hadn't seen it when I'd first come in.

'Dad?' I called him back. 'Where's Mum's painting?'

It had been in Mum's family for generations and was, she used to say proudly, worth a lot of money. But the money aspect wasn't important. At least, not to me and Liam. It was the link to Mum. We were just two months short of our tenth birthday when she died, and the stories she used to make up about the old-fashioned sailing ship and its adventures as it battled the stormy seas were among our most precious memories of her. Now all that was left was a light patch on the wall where the painting had been.

'Well, Dad, are you going to tell her? Or shall I?'

Archie went into overdrive at the sight of Liam, making the yowly-howly noise he does when he's excited. It's a weird, almost uncanny sound that makes you think of Dartmoor mists and Baskerville hounds and is a sort of cross between a bark, a howl and a yodel.

'Archie. Enough,' Liam said. The dog pressed as close as he could to Liam's leg and gazed up at him adoringly. But

Liam's eyes were firmly fixed on Dad, who stood as if turned to stone.

'Tell me what?' I asked, slightly panicked by the intense looks on their faces as they squared up to each other like a pair of fluffed-up pigeons. 'What is it?'

Dad looked away first. He turned to me. 'You see, the thing is, sweetheart . . . Your mother's picture. I had to sell it,' he said quietly. 'I had a few bills . . .'

Liam snorted. 'You mean you had nasty men banging on the door.'

'Oh no, Dad,' I began.

'Sure, your brother's exaggerating, as always. We've a temporary cash flow problem, that's all. That's why I couldn't make it to your graduation yesterday. I . . . I had to see the bank manager. In a bit of a hurry.' He looked down at his hands, his shoulders hunched, his voice so low I had to lean forward to hear him. 'If you must know, I'd very foolishly borrowed some money from these men and missed the repayment deadline — so they wanted it back. Soonest. And they weren't prepared to wait.'

I squeezed his hand, hating to see him look so defeated. Usually he could talk his way out of the tightest corner. But obviously not this time. 'It's OK, Dad. You don't have to say any more.'

'Yes he damn well does,' Liam cut in, the harshness of his voice making Archie look up at him, his amber eyes pools of anxiety. 'Tell her how you're gambling everything on a boat that was twenty years out of date before it hit the water. And while you're about it, why don't you tell her the name of the customer?'

'Be quiet, Liam,' Dad snapped, but Liam barrelled on.

'He can't, you see, Caitlin, because the customer insists on remaining anonymous — if you ever heard anything so outrageous. No name. No address. Nothing. But that's not the worst of it. Our mysterious customer very foolishly paid a wodge of money up front which, unfortunately, has been swallowed up in the black hole labelled 'Mulryan and Son overdraft'. So until we get some more cash from somewhere, Dad can't finish the boat. And until we finish the boat, we can't get the rest of our money. How's that for a vicious circle? And do you know the craziest thing of all? He turned down this really good offer . . . '

'That's enough,' Dad thundered. 'I'll not stay while the pair of you talk about me like I'm not here.'

If Mum's picture had been in its usual place, it would have fallen off the wall with the force with which he slammed the front door behind him as he stormed off. Archie whined anxiously while I glared at my twin. 'Why do you always wind him up like that?' I said.

But for once, Liam didn't laugh it off. 'I wasn't winding him up. I was merely stating the truth. Things really are bad, Cait. The boatyard's broke and the old fool's too stubborn to admit it.

He's been offered silly money for that patch of land out the back where the caravans used to be. It's nothing but an eyesore — but what does he do? Turns it down flat. Won't even discuss it with me. And we're supposed to be partners.'

I thought of Andrew Kington and his new project manager in his top-of-the-range look-at-me motor. 'The offer came from Andrew Kington, didn't it? For pity's sake, Liam. Of course he wouldn't accept it.'

5

'There,' Liam said. 'Do you see what I mean? It's ridiculous, the way he lives in the past. Whatever went down between him and Andrew Kington is history.'

'And, of course, you and Ben Kington are the best of buddies, aren't you? Like, you're not carrying on the family feud to the next generation,' I pointed out. 'Honestly, Liam, you're as bad as he is.'

'That's personal, between me and Ben. Nothing to do with our dads. Anyway, that's not the point. This is. Come with me.'

I followed him across the hall and into the dark little room Dad used as his office. Archie, who never wanted to let Liam out of his sight, padded along behind us, his claws clicking on the wooden floor.

Liam went across to the overflowing desk, picked up a sheaf of papers and handed them to me. 'Look, Cait, I don't have your flair for numbers, but even I can see these don't add up. See for yourself. Starting with the bank statements.'

I didn't have to look very far through the stack of final demands, threatening letters and overdrawn bank statements to see the truth in what Liam was saying. 'Jeez, this is terrible. I had no idea things were so bad,' I said.

'Mulryan and Son is finished,' he said curtly. 'We've got to move on. Which is exactly what I'm doing. You know I went to Poole this afternoon?'

'I'm hardly likely to forget, am I? Seeing as how you left me stranded at Dorchester.'

'Yeah, look, I'm really sorry about that. But it was the only way I could think of to get away for the afternoon without Dad going off on one.'

'Without telling him, you mean.'

He shrugged. 'Anyway, a mate gave

me an intro to this company in Poole. They design and build these amazing power boats. And guess what? They like my designs and want me to join their team.' He looked up at me, his face suddenly lighting up, his eyes shining. 'I still can't believe it. They're going to sponsor me through a design course at college and everything. Designing boats is the only thing I've ever wanted to do. It's the chance of a lifetime. I . . .'

He stopped at the sound of a boat engine starting up. We went outside in time to see an elegant blue and silver cabin cruiser pull away from the jetty and head out to sea, the engine noise sweet and throaty.

'Is that it?' I said, shielding my eyes as we watched the boat's clean lines as it sliced through the water, now streaked with gold from the setting sun. Behind it, the wake curved out in a graceful creamy white arc as the boat swept across the bay.

'Yeah,' Liam said. 'That's *Storm Chaser*.'

'The boat Dad's building for this mysterious client?'

'Who probably doesn't exist.'

'What?'

'Well, think about it, Cait. That's the boat he's always wanted to build. Always talked about building. I don't believe there ever was a mysterious anonymous client. I reckon Dad made that up, just so he could indulge his dream. There is no mystery customer, and that's why we're in this financial mess.'

'But the money up front — where did that come from?'

Liam shrugged. 'Probably had an insurance policy mature, won the lottery, who the hell knows? I'm only his business partner. I'm the last person he'd tell.'

'But the boat looks finished. Maybe he'll sell it, and — '

'It's finished, apart from the internal fittings. But he'll never sell it. He loves it. Believe me, I recognise the signs. This boat is the Special One.'

'It is beautiful,' I said, unable to take my eyes off it until it disappeared around the headland.

But Liam had already begun to walk away. 'Oh yes, it's beautiful,' he said, his voice edged with bitterness. 'In the way a lumbering old cart horse is. Give me a racehorse any day.'

'You're not really leaving the business, Liam, are you?' I asked as Archie and I hurried to keep up with him. 'It'll break Dad's heart.'

Liam spun round to face me, his eyes hot and angry, his hands balled into fists. 'Do you think I've not thought of that? That I haven't lain awake night after night thinking of little else? Of course he'll be upset. But it might be the jolt he needs to make him face reality. This place is going nowhere. Andrew Kington has plans to develop Stargate Bay as a marina. Think what that would do to the area.'

'A marina? So that's why he's employed this swanky new project manager.'

'How do you know that?' he asked.

'Because he was the guy who gave me a lift from Dorchester. Nick something. I can't remember if he told me his surname.'

'Nick Thorne. And he's OK.'

'So, is he the guy who's been badgering Dad?'

'Of course not. Although he was the one who approached Dad in the first place to make an offer on the old caravan field. An offer that Dad was more than happy to accept. He saw it as the solution to all our problems. Until, of course, he found out who Nick was working for.'

'Andrew Kington.'

'Yep. Then of course he turned it down flat. Wouldn't even consider it. Even though this marina could be the best thing to happen to Stargate in a long time.'

'Or the worst.'

'OK for you to go all sentimental about peace and quiet,' he flared, his temper never far from the surface, a sure sign of the stress he was under. 'You're the one who got away. So don't you dare lecture me on what I should or shouldn't do. I don't see you in any hurry to come back home and help out.'

That stung. Because, you see, I'd always envied Liam's relationship with Dad. It was like they were on the same wavelength while I was the odd one out. The oddball who got seasick, and preferred books to boats and maths to mackerel fishing.

'Look, I don't have to do my teacher training in September. I could — '

'Don't be ridiculous,' he snapped. 'I'm out of here.'

'Where are you going?' I called after him. 'I thought we were going to — '

'Got to go. Someone to see.' He jumped into his old pick-up and roared off.

'Welcome home, Caitlin,' I murmured as Archie nudged my hand. But even he was only after Maggie's chocolate cake, lying untouched on the kitchen table.

As I turned to go back into the house, I heard someone call my name. Maggie stood on the terrace of the tearoom, which was a little way down the road from our house. She beckoned me to join her.

'How did your graduation go?' she asked as Archie and I reached her. 'Your dad was terribly upset he couldn't make it. That's why I offered to go in his place.'

'Maggie, I'm so sorry.' I thought of the careless way I'd rejected her kind offer and how I'd regretted it the moment I'd done so.

'It's all right, lovey. I understand,' she said as she pushed a straying hairpin back in place. Liam always said Maggie had the look of an ageing hippie, with her long floaty clothes and mane of curly red hair that refused to stay put, no matter how many pins she jammed in it. She was sweet, funny, and the kindest person in the entire universe. Not to mention the best-ever baker of chocolate cake.

She'd been the one constant in my life. A lifelong friend of Mum's, she stepped in when Aunt Bridget, who'd never had the inclination to have children of her own, least of all put up with someone else's, gave up on us after a couple of years and went back to Ireland. Finding Liam's pet grass snake in her bed was, she told Dad, the final straw. And as for 'that lunatic dog, well, now don't get me started on that one'.

'Oh, you wouldn't have wanted me there, lovey, embarrassing you in front of all your smart university friends,' Maggie said as she avoided my eye by bending down to make a fuss of Archie.

I touched her shoulder. 'You would never do that, Maggie. I'd have loved you to have been there. I'm sorry; I was hurt and angry when Dad said he couldn't make it, and when he said you'd offered to come instead, I said no. Not that I didn't want you to come — I did. I was . . . ' I took a deep breath. This was really difficult. How could I explain it to her when I couldn't understand myself why I'd done it? 'I guess I was trying to make him feel so bad, he'd say he'd changed his mind and would come after all. I'm so sorry, Maggie. I behaved like a spoilt child who's just had her toys taken away. I really, really wished you'd been there.'

She straightened up, her face crumpled. 'Then I'm sorry I wasn't,' she said, blinking back tears and looking so upset, I wished I hadn't said anything.

'Unless, of course, you were going to pull the same stunt you did when I was in the under-15s hockey team and you whacked Jessica Simcox with your brolly.' I laughed in an attempt to lighten the moment.

'Serve the little minx right for cracking your shins like that,' she chuckled, and three more hairpins tinkled to the floor. Then with one of those jack-knife changes of subject she specialises in that always take me by surprise, she went on, 'Did you hear about poor old Sam?'

I thought of the gentle old man who'd lived in the bungalow next door for as long as I could remember, and my heart sank. 'Oh no. He's not . . .?'

'No, but he had a bad fall and has had to go into a nursing home. Poor love, couldn't cope on his own anymore. Andrew Kington was waving his chequebook as the ambulance drove away. You know he bought the pub a while back, don't you? I tell you, that man will own the whole place soon, except for your dad's place and mine.'

'So Dad was right about Andrew Kington's land grab, as he calls it.'

'He was. Not that I'm not likely to sell up and move from the place I've lived in all my life just so he can build his fancy marina.' She sniffed the air. 'Oh lord, that's my fruitcake. Must dash. And don't worry about yesterday. I'm sure you'll have some lovely pictures we can see.'

'I've ordered you a couple,' I said.

'Great.' She gave me a hug. 'Oh, it's so good to see you back home, lovey.

We'll have a good catch-up tomorrow, eh?'

Well, at least someone was glad I was back. I looked at Archie. He looked at me. 'So much for killing the fatted calf, eh?' I said to him, as I remembered what I'd said to Nick earlier.

But Archie wasn't interested in fatted calves. Only Maggie's chocolate cake that was calling him from the kitchen table.

6

Maggie was about to put the now-cooled fruitcake in the tin when she heard the throaty purr of Joe's boat as it came back across the bay, throttled back as if it were about to come in to the jetty, but then turned and headed back out to sea. She smiled as she traced its progress across the bay, watching until it disappeared around the headland, its sleek lines silhouetted against the setting sun. *Storm Chaser* was indeed a beautiful boat, and Joe had done a brilliant job on it. When he was on the boat all his troubles seemed to melt away, and he reminded Maggie of the happy-go-lucky young man who'd sailed into Stargate all those years ago. He'd been delivering a boat to her father, who back then had owned the boat yard. He'd fallen in love with the place and had never left. Never regretted it, either, so he said. Joe Mulryan had led a charmed life. That is, until Helen died. After that, nothing went right for him ever again.

Maggie cut a slice off the fruitcake. She'd meant to leave it, thinking she might open the tearoom tomorrow. But with the upset of Joe yesterday, and now Caitlin . . . She took a large bite and promised she'd think about the diet tomorrow.

Poor little Caitlin. Maggie felt really bad about not making it to her graduation yesterday, and wished she'd been a bit more forceful and not taken the first no for an answer. There was no excuse. She knew what Caitlin was like — always one to cut off her nose to spite her face, as Joe's sister Bridget always said.

But, if she were honest, she'd been quite relieved when Joe had said that Caitlin didn't want anyone there. It was the driving that did it. Ever since she'd had that little shunt on the dual carriageway last year, her confidence had taken a severe knock. She was all right about driving into Bridport to do the shopping, but the thought of driving any further filled her with dread. As for going all the way to Exeter and dealing with that terrible junction just off the motorway by the services there . . . her heart lurched at the thought of it.

Besides, she wasn't any good at this socialising malarkey, and was well aware that people thought she was a bit weird. Although if she'd realised that Caitlin needed her, she wouldn't have cared what people thought. Or about the driving. She'd have even made an effort to dress normally for once. If only she'd known. *If only* — her old dad used to say they were the two saddest words in the English language. And he wasn't wrong. If that wasn't the story of her life, eh? Littered with if onlys.

Maggie took another bite of the fruitcake and went back to her book. Soon she was engrossed in the heroine's struggle to overcome her problems. The world of fiction was much less complicated than the real world.

* * *

How sad was that, being home alone on my first evening back? I put Maggie's untouched cake away, then fed the dog his regular food. He was totally unimpressed and kept looking from his bowl up to the kitchen table then back to his bowl, as if he thought the cake would somehow miraculously reappear and find its way there.

'Live with it, dog,' I told him. 'Looks like we're both destined to be disappointed this evening.'

I considered sitting down to watch the early-evening news, but thought better of it. I contemplated eating Maggie's cake in one sitting, but thought better of that, too. Then I remembered Nick's casual comment that he might look in at the Sailor's that evening.

I grabbed my coat and was almost

out of the door when I caught sight of myself in the hall mirror, still in the same scruffy jeans and crumpled T-shirt I'd put on this morning. I put my coat down, went upstairs and changed into a slightly less scruffy pair of jeans and a cashmere jumper in a soft sugared-almond pink that Maggie had given me for Christmas.

I brushed my wild curls into submission and pinned them at the nape of my neck. Then I took extra care over my make-up, carefully concealing the freckles on my nose. A touch of eyeshadow, a flick of lipstick and I felt — and looked — a whole lot better. I'd been saving the jumper for a special occasion, and a quick drink in the Sailor's wasn't exactly that. But I needed cheering up, and who knew who might be there. Maybe even Nick.

* * *

He wasn't. But Ben Kington was. Hunched over the bar, the frown on his face changed to a lazy, heart-stopping smile as he saw me. 'Well, well, well. If it isn't our resident maths genius,' he drawled, his slightly slurred words indicating he'd been there some time.

'Yeah, well, sorry about that,' I mumbled. 'I . . . um . . . thought Liam might be here?'

Ben swivelled on his stool and looked around the dimly lit bar with its nicotine-stained ceilings and faded prints advertising beers that hadn't been available since the start of the Second World War. The place was empty except for a couple of wizened old men hunched over their game of dominoes in the far corner.

'Nope. Can't see him,' he said.

'Oh, right. Then I'll just . . . ' I turned to leave but he put his hand out. Shockwaves zipped through my body at the touch of his long, tanned fingers on my wrist.

'You're looking good tonight, Caitlin,' he said, and I blessed the impulse that had made me go upstairs and change. This was definitely a pink cashmere jumper moment. 'Fancy a drink to celebrate your homecoming? What will it be?'

I thought of the empty house waiting for me. Of Dad and Liam and all that mess. Of Ben Kington offering to buy me a drink. No contest.

'Thanks. I'll have a vodka and Coke, please.' I hauled myself up onto the stool beside him and picked up the glass, ice chinking as I did so. I was aiming for the cool and sophisticated look, but inside my heart was pounding away like a jackhammer. 'Cheers.'

'Welcome home, Caitlin.' He made my name sound so smooth and sensual, it sent a shiver down my spine.

'Thanks. It's good to be home.' My throat had gone dry and my voice came out all wrong — a strangled squawk when I'd been trying for a sultry purr. I took a large gulp of my drink and ended up with a mouthful of ice cubes. So much for cool and sophisticated.

'So, tell me, did you enjoy your ride

in Nick Thorne's flash motor?'

I crunched the last of the ice, swallowed quickly and shook my head. 'Nothing changes around here, does it?' I said, relieved to find my voice had returned to normal. 'You can't sneeze without everyone passing comment.'

'Tell me about it.' He leaned towards me, his handsome face suddenly serious. He looked like he was trying to make up his mind about something. 'Caitlin. There's something . . . no, hang on a minute. Ready for another?'

'I'm OK, thanks.' My glass was still half-full, but he got me another anyway. 'Thanks. What were you going to say?'

'I like you, Caitlin — which is why I'm telling you this. So hear me out and please don't jump down my throat.'

I finished the first glass and put it to one side, giving a nervous laugh. 'You're making it sound quite serious. Should I be worried?'

'Not worried. I just wanted to put you on your guard, that's all. Nick Thorne asked you out, didn't he?'

I jerked back as if stung, my face burning. This conversation was not exactly going the way I'd hoped. 'Well, no. Not really. It was just . . . you know,' I floundered around, embarrassed and awkward, as 'cool and sophisticated' vanished like a snowflake on a bonfire. 'I may have said 'see you around later' or something. Just one of those things you say. Casual, like. Not a date or anything like that.'

'That's as may be. But Dad and I both heard you saying something to Thorne about the possibility of meeting up for a drink later. It was a short hop from there to Dad saying to him about chatting you up, to see if he could find out Joe's position on the land deal through you.'

'You're joking.' I couldn't believe what I was hearing. But Ben didn't look like he was joking. He looked deadly serious. 'Surely your father wouldn't do something so . . . so underhand?'

'He's determined this marina is going

to go ahead and right now. Your dad's the only thing standing in his way.'

'But Nick? Surely he wouldn't go along with it,' I said, but a little worm of doubt was already beginning to wriggle its way around my mind. He had, after all, been pretty quick to ask me out, hadn't he? Once he'd found out I was Joe Mulryan's daughter. And I, idiot that I was, had been flattered, thinking it was my irresistible charm he'd succumbed to.

Ben tossed back his drink. 'As you say, it's a pretty underhand thing to do. But that's what Thorne's like, and why I wanted to warn you. In the short time he's been here, he's managed to sideline me good and proper. Dad's always banging on about Nick says this, Nick does that. It really winds me up, I can tell you.'

'Yes, I can see that,' I murmured, not really paying much attention to what he said as my mind was still reeling.

'I also think it's despicable when an incomer starts stirring up the old feud between our two families, don't you?' Ben went on.

'I certainly do.' How stupid was I? How could I have been so wrong about a man? I'd thought Nick Thorne was a really nice guy. Showed what I knew, didn't it? No wonder I was off men for life — with the exception of Ben, of course. I picked up my glass, surprised to find it was almost empty again.

He motioned to the barman for another round, then smiled at me. 'Do you know, Caitlin, this thing between our families — it's pathetic, isn't it? What say we're the first to ditch the stupid feud? Here's to peace breaking out between us.'

'I'll drink to that,' I said.

So we did. Several times. In fact, it got to the stage where I forgot I hadn't eaten since a soggy egg sandwich at Exeter station. I forgot about the row between Dad and Liam and that the family business was in serious financial trouble. I even forgot I was trying to be cool and sophisticated.

But I did not forget that Nick Thorne had asked me out so he could pump me for information about my dad.

7

Nick parked the car and sat there for several minutes before getting out. What the heck was he doing here? He'd promised himself there was no way he was going to The Sailor's Return that evening. There were at least a dozen pubs in the wider area he could have chosen — nicer pubs with better beer, and menus that were a little more sophisticated than pickled eggs and peanuts. The pub didn't even have a sea view, except from the upstairs storeroom window. Andrew had plans for gutting the place and turning the first floor into a large open-plan dining room, which made a lot of sense. But whether he'd get a return on his investment was another matter. Probably not, if his plans for the marina didn't go through.

Maybe while he was here in Stargate

he'd take another look at the site of the old bungalow Andrew had just bought and see if he could come up with an alternative access that didn't involve Joe Mulryan's property. Nick remembered the look in Joe's eyes when he'd told him he was working for Andrew Kington. There was no way on earth Joe was ever going to sell that piece of land to him. 'Hell will freeze over before I do,' he'd said — or words to that effect. Which was why Nick had been thinking about alternative access. But first, that pint was calling him. And if Caitlin and her brother were in the bar, well, that would be fine. It wasn't like he'd come here looking for her or anything daft like that. He just happened to be in the area, that was all.

He pushed open the door that led into the public bar, which at first sight appeared empty. But as his eyes became accustomed to the gloom, he could see two old men in the far corner and a couple sitting at the bar. At first he thought it was Caitlin and Liam and was about to go up and join them, when he realised his mistake. It was Caitlin, all right — there was no mistaking those long, slender legs, and she'd done something to her mop of curls that really suited her. But the man with her, draped all over her like a rash, was none other than the boss's son.

Nick turned and left quickly before anyone saw him. Not that there was any danger of that. The barman was nowhere to be seen — and Ben and Caitlin were so engrossed in each other, a troop of marines could have yomped through the bar singing 'Colonel Bogey' and they wouldn't have noticed.

Ben and Caitlin. Who'd have thought it? Nick thought she'd have had more sense than to fall for a spoilt brat like Ben Kington — a guy who thought the normal rules of life didn't apply to him.

It was stupid of him to feel so annoyed and let down. After all, it hadn't been a firm commitment, just a vague 'if you happen to be around' sort of thing.

Well, he wasn't around. He was out of here. He'd had enough of Stargate Bay for one day. He wrenched open the car door and, promising himself he'd come back tomorrow to check out the bungalow site, drove back to his hotel. Suddenly an evening full of paperwork seemed very appealing.

* * *

'Who was that?' I had my back to the door, but the rush of air as it closed caused a curled-up poster advertising a long-gone car boot sale to slide off the wall and land at my feet.

Ben looked over my shoulder and smiled. 'No one,' he said. 'Well, no one we need to bother about anyway. Now, where were we? Oh yes — I remember. We were drinking to peace breaking out between our families, weren't we?'

Yes. Of course we were. Peace and love. That was what it was all about, wasn't it? I was relaxed, happy and in love with the world as all my worries drifted away like the morning mist.

By the end of the evening, even the revelation about Nick Thorne's treachery ceased to rankle, and everything merged into a glorious, vodka-fuelled fug of happiness as Ben and I discovered we had more in common than we'd ever realised, including fathers who didn't appreciate us.

I can't tell you what else we talked about because, to be honest, it didn't make much sense at the time, least of all the next morning. Except to say that as the evening wore on, we really did see ourselves as some kind of latter-day Romeo and Juliet.

'The two star-crossed lovers of Stargate Bay,' I giggled, and really believed that was the wittiest, cleverest remark ever.

'Star-crossed lovers, eh?' Ben said. 'I like the sound of that. Can I walk you home, Miss Mulryan?'

'I rather think you'd better, Mr Kington. Something weird is happening to the ground this evening. It keeps moving up and down. Can't you feel it?'

Once outside and with Ben's arm around my shoulders, the ground began to steady up. Our walk took us via the beach, where the moon shimmered on the water and Stargate Bay looked soft, romantic, and more beautiful than I'd ever seen it.

Who could blame us for sitting down on the beach and listening to the hypnotic rhythm of the waves lapping the shore while the moon bathed everything in liquid silver? OK, so the horizon wouldn't stay still, tilting alarmingly if I looked at it too long; and when I tried to skim a pebble across the water — something I am usually amazingly good at — it sank without trace.

'Go on then,' I said as Ben laughed at my efforts. 'You see if you can do any better.'

'Oh, I rather think I can. I can do a whole lot better than that,' he said, his face suddenly serious as he took the pebble I offered him, tossed it away and gently pushed me back onto the pebbles.

My heart was pounding, my mouth dry. And I was clean out of things to say.

'I think I'm falling in love with you, Caitlin Mulryan,' he whispered as he leaned over and kissed me.

A cloud rolled across the moon and a breeze sprang up, bringing fresh, chilly air in off the sea. The pebbles were cold and sharp against my back. But I didn't care. Nothing mattered except that single, unbelievable miracle. Ben said he loved me. He really, truly loved me. My wildest dream had come true.

I shivered and he pulled me closer. Ben and me. Here on the beach. Together. After tonight, nothing would ever be the same.

* * *

'Where the hell have you been?' Liam asked when, after a couple of failed attempts, I finally got the key in the lock and let myself, stumbling, into the house.

'I've been . . . with someone who app-appreciates me,' I giggled as the words tangled around my tongue. 'Some lovely someone who thinks I'm . . . the . . . the brightest star in Stargate Bay, and — '

'You're totally wasted, you lightweight,' he laughed. 'Never could hold your drink, could you? Go on up before Dad comes home. I'll cover for you.'

'So, so kind, brother dear,' I said, weaving my way towards the stairs. 'I'll do the same for you one day. Oh no, I already have, haven't I? Last Christmas — or was it the Christmas before? — when you — '

'Go to bed, Cait. Dad will be back any minute. Do you need a hand?'

'Of course not. I'm perfect . . . perfectly all right, thank you very much. Oh, and by the way, you'll be glad to hear we — my star-crossed lover and I — have decided to put an end to all this nonsense between our families.'

'What?' Liam came across to me, all laughter gone now as he grabbed me by the shoulders, his fingers digging in. 'Who did you say you'd been with?'

'Get off, you great oaf. You're hurting me,' I said as I shook myself free.

'Who have you been with, Caitlin?'

'Not that it's any of your business,' I said, rubbing my shoulder, 'but I've been with Ben Kington. He's not the monster you and Dad make him out to be, you know. Not when you get to know him. He's really, really sweet and kind, and — '

Liam swore. 'For pity's sake, are you mad? You know it was him who put the heavies on Dad the other day, don't you? You didn't tell him anything?'

'Tell him what?'

'About the business not doing so well. Stuff like that.'

'Of course I didn't. Besides, we had better things to talk about. And laugh about. He's really, really funny. And he

. . . he loves me.'

'Yeah, right. Of course he does.' He put his arm around me. 'Cait, that guy only loves one person, and that's himself. You didn't . . . ?'

I didn't want to hear this. 'I'm not going to stand here while you lecture me like you've suddenly turned into Aunt Bridget,' I said as I pushed him away.

If only I'd lied to him; told him nothing happened between me and Ben. That we'd had a couple of drinks together before going our separate ways.

But I didn't. Instead I staggered up the stairs, already feeling bad about what had happened. I'm not that kind of girl, honestly. I don't do one-night stands. But it was Ben and, as I've already said, he was the exception to every rule in my book. Even that one. Besides, he loved me, didn't he? And I really, really hoped that for him, like me, it had been more than a one-night stand.

Nevertheless, I thought it would be sensible to go into town first thing, find myself a chemist where nobody knew me, and ask for the morning-after pill.

8

Nick had been in the office for over an hour, Andrew even longer, when Ben strolled in. His sullen expression turned to a full-on scowl as his father pointedly looked up at the clock.

'What time do you call this?' Andrew demanded. 'If you got home at a decent hour . . . '

'For pity's sake, spare me the lecture, Dad,' Ben growled, making straight for the coffee machine. 'I've got a bad enough headache as it is.'

'OK, well now you're here, pull up a chair. Nick's just about to go through his report on his meeting in London yesterday.'

'Do I have to?' Ben tossed back the coffee, grimacing at the taste. 'Nothing I say will make a blind bit of difference. The two of you will already have made up your minds about it. I only came in to get the keys. I thought I'd take the boat out for a spin; blow away the cobwebs. And get myself some decent coffee while I'm at it.'

'Blow away the hangover, more like,' Andrew said. 'For heaven's sake, boy, when are you going to grow up?'

Ben whipped round, his fists clenched, his eyes hot and angry. 'How about when you stop calling me 'boy'? And stop treating me like I'm ten years old.'

'How about you stop *acting* like you're ten years old?' Andrew said as he stormed out of the office, the tasteful prints on the wall rattling as he slammed the door behind him.

Nick looked down at his desk and carried on working, aware that Ben was watching him closely, the expression on his face suggesting he was looking for a fight. Well, he could carry on looking. Nick had no intention of rising to the bait. He liked his job; it was stretching him in a way he hadn't been stretched for a long time. It felt surprisingly good to be back in harness again, and he wasn't going to jeopardise that by having a fight with the boss's spoilt brat of a son.

'I told her, you know,' Ben said, his thumbs hooked into his belt, a smug grin on his face.

Nick looked up. 'Told who what?'

'Dad asked you to chat up Caitlin Mulryan, didn't he? To find out what that fool of a father of hers was up to. Don't try to deny it, because I heard him.'

'Then you will also have heard me refuse,' Nick said quietly.

'Hah! So he did ask you.' Ben gave a crow of triumph. 'I knew it. I know the old man so well. The minute I saw you roll up with Joe Mulryan's daughter, I could see what was going through his mind. Never could pass up a chance to get one over on Joe Mulryan, could Dad. And I was right, wasn't I?'

'I told you,' Nick said with the exaggerated patience people usually reserve for talking to a three-year-old.

'Your father did indeed ask me to try and find out what Joe Mulryan was up to via his daughter; you're right about that. But, like I said, I refused.'

Ben snorted. 'Yeah, right. And Dad takes a refusal so well, doesn't he? Anyway, last night I told Caitlin that's why you asked her out. She wasn't too happy, I can tell you. Oh dear, I hope I haven't messed things up for you,' he added, although the tone of his voice suggested that he very much hoped the opposite.

There was a sudden unexpected crack. Nick looked down and saw that the pencil he'd been holding had snapped beneath the pressure of his tightly clenched fingers. He tossed both ends in the bin. 'No doubt you consoled her,' Nick said curtly.

'Oh yes, I consoled her all right,' Ben drawled with a grin. 'But then, you saw us, didn't you? You were going into the Sailor's to do my father's bidding, in spite of your holier-than-thou denial — and, what do you know, I got there before you. I'm very good at consoling, you know. Well, let's put it this way — Caitlin wasn't complaining.'

Ben took a step backwards as Nick stood up, his chair screeching against the wooden floor. 'I've got to go out for a while,' he said. 'I'll catch you later, Ben.'

As he left the office, he reminded himself why he had taken this job — how much it was helping him put his life back together again; how much he needed it. He weighed all that against the overwhelming urge to wipe that supercilious smile off Ben Kington's face once and for all.

The job, and common sense, won — this time.

* * *

As I drifted off to sleep last night, I'd been full of plans, short- and long-term. Long-term — well, that was all Ben. But in the short term, maybe a walk along the cliffs with the dog, hopefully with Ben if he was around. We both loved the view from the top of Golden Cap, the highest point on the south coast. It was yet another thing we'd discovered we had in common, and I had vague memories of us saying something about meeting up, although I couldn't quite remember what we'd arranged. I'd phone him later and find out.

But first, though, I was going to make that trip into town for the morning-after pill. I wasn't even going to tell him about it. Our relationship was, I felt, way too young to cope with an unplanned pregnancy. And so, I reckoned, was I.

But in the end I did none of these things.

Instead I woke next morning to one of those head-splitting 'never again' headaches and the sound of raised voices coming from the direction of the boat house. I groaned. Dad and Liam were obviously having yet another set-to. But when I got up and looked out of the window, I saw Dad's van had gone, and I heard a voice I recognised. My heart leapt. It was Ben's.

Ben, here already. How keen was that? I looked across to the jetty and, sure enough, there tied up to one of the mooring posts was Ben's boat. Liam had described *Storm Chaser* as a cart horse, which was pretty mean of him. Ben's boat, however, was one hundred per cent pure thoroughbred racehorse. With powerful twin outboard engines, and its mirror-black finish emblazoned with vivid crimson flashes, it looked — and was — built for one thing: speed. It was Ben's newest toy and, as he'd told me last night, the love of his life.

'After you, of course,' he'd added with that slow, heart-stopping smile that melted my bones.

I grabbed the first pair of jeans I came to but decided against the pink cashmere sweater, tossed carelessly over the back of a chair from last night. Instead, I pulled on a T-shirt, dashed down a couple of paracetamol, and hurried out to the boat house with Archie padding along at my heels like a shadow. I couldn't wait to see Ben again.

'People who listen at keyholes never hear any good of themselves,' Aunt Bridget used to say.

Oh, how I wish I'd listened to her. Just that once. But I didn't. Instead, I paused at the door to the boat house, my attention caught by Liam's angry voice. He was telling Ben to lay off Dad. Now, surely, Ben would deny having anything to do with the heavies who had paid Dad a visit the other day. Now he would tell Liam what he'd told me last night — that he had absolutely no idea who those men were. And that he would be having stern words with his father as soon as possible.

'How many times do I have to spell it out, Mulryan?' Ben sounded as angry as Liam, and who could blame him in the face of Liam's unfair accusation? 'If a man can't pay his debts, that's his problem. Not mine. And if my friends upset your old man the other day, well, that's too bad as well. Maybe next time the stubborn old fool will pay up on time.'

I jumped back from the door as if it had suddenly become white-hot. What was Ben saying? I'd expected him to deny it. To tell Liam how he'd got it all wrong. Instead — had he really called my dad a stubborn old fool who'd got what he deserved? I couldn't believe it.

'You're nothing but a thug,' Liam said, and I didn't have to see his face to know he was having a hard time hanging on to his temper. I could hear it in his voice. I was about to go in when I heard my name. And froze.

'You reckon? A thug, eh? Well, that wasn't what Caitlin called me last night,' Ben said with a snigger that made my flesh crawl. 'More stud than thug, I think you'll find. In fact, she said that I — '

'You leave my sister out of this.'

'Too late, I'm afraid. I had her, Mulryan. Out there on the beach, just outside your pathetic, falling-down boatyard. I had your sister. And why not? I reckoned I'd get payment out of the Mulryan family one way or another. And she was well up for it, I can tell you. I didn't have to force her.'

I wanted to cover my ears. To block out his cruel words. To run away from the sound of his mocking voice. But I did none of those things. Instead, I stood there, clutching Archie's collar as if it was a lifebelt and I was a drowning rat, while Ben went on. And on. Like he was enjoying himself.

'And what do you know?' he was saying. 'Clever little Caitlin came up trumps and delivered on time, unlike her old man. She helped pass what otherwise would have been a very boring evening.'

How could I have been so dumb? So pathetically naive? Stupid. Stupid. Stupid. I'd believed him when he said he loved me, yet here he was boasting about it. Using the fact that we'd made love to bait my brother. He saw it as nothing more than payment of the family debt, and a way to pass an otherwise boring evening. When all the time I thought he loved me, like I loved him. Like I'd loved him all my life. But not anymore. How could I have been so stupid as to think that Ben Kington loved me?

I felt sick, used, and dirty. I wanted to run back indoors, get under a hot shower, and stay there for the rest of the day. The rest of my life, even, given half a chance.

But as I turned to go, I heard the sounds of a scuffle. A sickening thud. Then a brief, scary silence. Before I could move, the boat house door was wrenched open. Liam raced across to the jetty. Leapt into *Storm Chaser*. Started the engine. Roared off.

He was in such a state, he didn't see me. He didn't see Archie either, racing off towards the jetty after him. But I had seen the wild, frightened look on my brother's face.

I'd seen, too, the bloody handprint on the boat house door, where he'd pushed it open.

9

Ben lay face down on the floor. Blood, vivid crimson against the dusty concrete, pooled at his right temple. He wasn't moving. There was a smear of blood on the sharp corner of the workbench. Ben had obviously cracked his head on it as he fell.

'Oh no. Dear God, no.' I was angry with him, more angry than I'd ever been in my life. Hurt beyond measure. Humiliated. Betrayed. But I hadn't wanted this. Not this.

'Oh Liam, Liam,' I whispered. 'What have you done?'

I knelt down beside Ben and tried to remember how to find a pulse. How to do CPR. What to do? Should I move him? Call for an ambulance? Run for help? *Think, Caitlin, think. Swallow down the panic that's threatening to engulf you and think.*

And then, to my intense relief, he began to stir. Just his arms at first, his hands pressing onto the hard floor. He gave a low, soft moan, then swore loudly and fiercely. It was the best sound I had ever heard.

'Ben? Ben, are you all right?' I put a hand on his shoulder. 'Don't try and sit up. I'll call an ambulance.'

He swore again as he put his hand to his temple, then looked down at the blood on his fingers.

'I don't need an ambulance,' he said, and I was relieved to see the colour returning to his face.

I helped him to his feet. My hands were still shaking as I took a clean tissue from my pocket and began to clear what appeared, thankfully, to be a superficial wound just above his right eye. The cut was long but not deep, and he had the beginnings of a spectacular bruise.

'You Mulryans.' He swotted my hand away. 'You're raving mad, the whole damn lot of you.'

'You and Liam were fighting.'

'I wasn't fighting. It was your moronic brother. I'd lost a fender and came down to see if he could sell me one. But he just went off on one. Making all sort of wild accusations. Then, out of the blue, he took a swing at me.'

I wanted to say that I knew what they'd been arguing about. That I'd overheard everything. But I didn't get the chance. He was beyond angry. Beyond reason. There was a look in his eyes that made me step away from him. He was a wild-eyed stranger. It was impossible to believe he was the same man I'd sat on the beach with last night counting the stars.

'He'll be more than sorry when I catch up with him,' he snarled. 'Nobody, but nobody, puts me on the floor, least of all a Mulryan. He caught me unawares, that was all.'

'Don't, Ben,' I pleaded, suddenly feeling very scared for my brother. 'Remember, last night, we said it was time to end the feud between our families?'

His laugh sent a shiver crawling down my spine. 'You're not nearly as clever as everyone says, are you, Caitlin Mulryan? Like I told your brother just now, last night was payment of a family debt. Nothing more. Time to end the family feud? Fancy clever little Caitlin falling for that.'

'Ben, please don't.' I couldn't bear to hear any more.

'Got to go. I've given him and his old bath tub enough of a head start now.'

'Ben, stop!' I cried as I raced after him. He was making for the jetty where Archie stood, tail down, shoulders hunched as he watched Liam heading out to sea.

'Please, Ben. Wait. Just calm down for a minute. Please don't.' My pleas became more desperate, my cries louder. But he ignored them all.

I reached the jetty just as he untied the mooring rope and jumped into his boat. The engines screamed into ear-splitting life, drowning out the last of my cries. I could only stand with Archie and watch, helpless and terrified, as the boat roared away, crashing and bumping across the waves with a force that must have shaken his bones.

He caught up with Liam in no time and they raced alongside each other, although Ben's faster boat could have pulled away at any time. But he didn't. Instead, it seemed to me that he was taunting Liam.

'Liam, turn round! Come back!' I cried, even though I knew he couldn't hear me.

Then it happened. Over in a split second, yet played out in what seemed to be unbearably slow freeze-frame motion. One boat — I think it was Ben's, because I'm almost sure I saw a flash of red — suddenly reared up like a startled horse. Hung as if suspended in mid-air. Crashed down on top of the other.

Frame by frame, I saw tongues of

flame swirl and dance among splinters of wreckage like some ghastly firework display. Burning fragments shot high into the air before raining down onto the water.

It seemed like the sea itself was on fire.

10

The dog was there again at the end of the jetty, staring out to sea with that patient, half-zonked expression dogs specialise in. He was waiting, like he always did whenever Liam took the boat out. But the sight of him sitting there was breaking my heart, because of course Liam wasn't coming home again. Ever.

But Archie didn't understand that. He was only a dog, and not a very bright one at that.

'The poor old fellow's still doing it then?' Maggie said, coming up quietly behind me.

'Every day,' I sighed. 'It's been over a week now. He'd stay there all day and all night too if I let him. He's not eating properly either.'

A couple of hairpins tinkled unnoticed onto the pebbles as Maggie shook her head. 'And what about you and Joe, lovey?' she asked gently. 'Did either of you manage any of that casserole I made for you yesterday?'

'It was lovely, thanks.' I thought of the casserole, lying untouched on the kitchen table. But it wasn't a complete lie, as Maggie's casseroles are always lovely. And I didn't want to hurt her feelings. It was such a kind gesture. So typical of Maggie. 'But Dad.' I swallowed hard. 'I'm worried sick about him, Maggie. He's not eating at all, and I know he's not sleeping much either. But he says he's fine and I'm not to fuss. Then he goes out, like he's done every day since the accident. I've asked him where he goes but he just says 'here and there', like it's none of my business.'

'Would you like me to have a word with him?' Maggie asked.

'You can try, but you know what he's like.'

'As in stubborn, opinionated, and too damn independent for his own good?'

'That's my dad.' I almost managed a smile. 'Well, I'd better go and get Archie before the rain comes. See if I can tempt him to eat . . . ' I almost said 'with leftover casserole' but stopped myself in time.

'Poor Joe,' she sighed as she walked across the beach with me, our footsteps crunching across the pebbles. 'In a way, it's worse for him than for Andrew. At least Andrew can plan Ben's funeral, get some sort of closure, mourn him properly. But for Joe . . . '

'That's the worst of it. To start with, he refused to believe Liam was dead. But now we wake up every morning wondering if today's going to be the day the wreckage from the boat — or . . . or Liam's body turns up. It's the not knowing that's so unbearable. Every time the phone rings, or there's a knock at the door . . . '

Suddenly the dog leapt up, ears pricked, tail wagging, at the sound of a boat engine. But it was only a fishing boat following a shoal of mackerel, so

Archie went back to his vigil.

I shivered as a herring gull wheeled overhead, outstretched wings brilliant white against the darkening sky. Its mournful shrieks reminded me of how Liam and I used to scare the bejesus out of each other when we were little with stories of how they were the souls of the dead, crying out.

I couldn't stand this. Ben. Liam. The accident. Dad. The business. Ben's heavies. And now poor old Archie, waiting for a boat that would never come home.

I couldn't keep it to myself any longer. Maggie had always been a good listener, and her gentle common sense had seen me through many teenage traumas.

But this was not about an outbreak of spots or not being picked for the hockey team. This was in a different league altogether.

I turned to look at Maggie and took a deep breath. She was going to hate me when I told her, but it couldn't be helped. I had to tell someone or I'd explode. I started with the easy bit.

'Dad's got serious money problems,' I began. 'The business is in real financial difficulties. He and Liam . . . well, let's say they couldn't agree on how best to deal with it; only of course it was a bit more than that. Liam said there'd been some heavies banging on the door, but Dad said he was exaggerating as always. They had a big falling-out about it the day I came home.'

Maggie's face went the colour of cold porridge. 'The heavies? Would that be the day before your graduation?'

'Possibly. Dad's excuse for not coming was that he had to see the bank manager in a hurry.'

'Oh Lord, I saw them. As unsavoury a pair as I've seen outside an episode of *Doctor Who*. I was out on the terrace and they asked me where Mulryan and Son was. I pretended not to know, but then one of them spotted the sign on the boatyard entrance. I've been worrying about it ever since, but your dad was very cagey when I asked him about it. Who were they and what did they want?'

'According to Liam, Ben Kington sent them. Dad had borrowed some money and they came to collect, or else. Liam says . . . ' I broke off as a wave of nausea swept over me. 'Liam said,' I corrected myself miserably, then blurted out, 'Oh Maggie, it's all my fault. It's my fault he's dead.'

There. I'd said it aloud. The thing that had been eating me up inside and robbed me of sleep for the last week. Now all I had to do was tell Maggie what had happened between Ben and Liam and watch the sympathy in her eyes drain away.

'I keep trying to find the courage to tell Dad what really happened,' I hurried on before Maggie could interrupt. 'Ben and Liam had a fight in the boat house. Liam hit Ben, then jumped into *Storm Chaser* and took off. Ben came round and went after him like a bat out of hell. I — I lied to the police.

At least, I didn't tell them about the fight. Just said I thought they were racing and there was an accident.'

The scene played out in my head, over and over on a continuous loop, as it had every day since the accident.

'But they weren't racing. Well, they were, but not in a good way. It was about me — the fight. The accident was all my fault.'

'How do you make that out? Those boys were fighting ever since they were old enough to shake a rattle at each other.'

'But this time was different, Maggie.' I rammed my fists into my jeans pocket and forced myself to look at her, even though I didn't want to see the look of disgust and disapproval that would flash upon her face when I told her. 'They were fighting over me. Ben and I . . . we had a bit of a . . . ' I took a deep, steadying breath. 'You won't know this, but I've always had a bit of a thing about Ben. And the night I came home, Dad and Liam had a row; they both stormed off in a huff and I was on my own. So . . . so I went to the pub, and there was Ben. We had a few drinks together, and he was very sweet and kind.'

I broke off. Because of course, he wasn't being sweet or kind. 'I had her, Mulryan.' I could still hear Ben's voice, boasting to Liam. I shuddered and closed my eyes briefly, in a futile attempt to shut the image out.

'You don't have to say any more, lovey,' Maggie said. 'And I knew how you felt about Ben. I could see it in your face every time you saw him or talked about him. And if you and him had some moments of happiness together before he died, well, that's something to treasure, isn't it? To help you through the sadness of losing him.'

The sadness of losing him? Maggie thought I was grieving for Ben — the man who was responsible for the death of my brother? Whatever I imagined I'd felt for Ben had been killed that morning in the boat house.

Only of course it wasn't just Ben who was responsible for Liam's death. I was, too. If I hadn't been so stupid, so naive.

'And if Liam didn't approve of you and Ben,' Maggie was saying, 'then that was his problem, not yours.'

'Yes, but I shouldn't have . . . '

Maggie gripped my shoulders, her expression fierce. 'Now you listen to me, young lady. None of this was your fault. If anyone other than Ben and Liam are to blame for the accident, then it's Andrew and Joe.'

'But if I hadn't . . . '

'But nothing,' she interrupted firmly. 'Your father and Andrew have let this ridiculous feud go on long enough. It was all so long ago now. If your mother was still alive, she'd be furious with the pair of them. I've kept out of it long enough. And got my head bitten off by your father if I as much suggested he should put an end to it. But I'll not stand by and see you blame yourself for something that started long before you were born.'

11

Maggie was shocked at the bleak despair in Caitlin's eyes. 'Come over here, lovey, and let's sit down and have a chat.' She led her across to a flat rock that had always been a favourite picnic spot when Caitlin and Liam had been little.

Caitlin sat down, pulled her knees up to her chest and wrapped her too-thin arms around them as if she were cold, even though the air was oppressively warm and heavy with the stillness that precedes a storm. 'Tell me about the feud, Maggie. I know you've always said it's not your story to tell; that I should ask Dad. But every time Liam or I tried, he'd just go off on one about Andrew Kington being nothing more than a crook, then say it all happened a long time ago and these things are best forgotten.'

But they weren't forgotten, Joe, were they? Maggie thought. *And that's what's caused the haunted look in your daughter's eyes, and the fact that she blames herself for the boys' deaths. When, of course, it wasn't her fault at all. It was yours and Andrew's. Although, to be fair, the fault was mostly Andrew's.*

'Do you know what started it?' Caitlin asked. 'You and Mum were at school together, weren't you? So you must have been around at the time.'

'Oh yes, I was around at the time.' Maggie thought carefully about what she was going to say. Caitlin needed to hear the truth, or at least some of it, if only to give her something else to think about. But where to start? What to say? And, the most difficult of all, what to leave unsaid?

'All we knew was that Dad and Andrew had been sniping away at each other for as long as we could remember,' Caitlin went on. 'But it got a lot worse after Mum died. I suppose she wasn't around to keep them in check.'

'Something like that.' Maggie fixed her eyes on Archie, who now lay with his head on his paws, his ears still pricked as he stared out to sea where the gathering storm clouds blotted out the horizon.

If Liam was still around, there was no way she'd say anything; Liam had been as hot-headed as Joe, and all it would have done was make a bad situation worse. But Caitlin was different. She took after her mother. In fact, she was growing more like Helen every day. Even down to the way she laughed, the way she chewed her thumbnail when she was anxious, the way she fretted about the freckles on her nose. So very much like Helen. If her hair was shorter — Helen had worn hers in a boyish crop, which suited her elfin features — the resemblance would be quite striking. It must give Joe — and maybe Andrew too, come to that — quite a jolt to see it.

'All Mum ever said was that the two of them needed to grow up, which as young children we always found hilarious,' Caitlin said. 'And if we asked Dad, he'd just say Andrew Kington was a crook and his son was no better. I know you always said it wasn't your story to tell, but . . . '

'But that was before their stupid squabbling cost them both their sons,' Maggie said fiercely. 'And I'll not have you blame yourself for that.'

'So what were they squabbling about?'

Maggie picked up a smooth, flat pebble and sent it skimming across the water with a skill born of a lifetime of practice. 'What you need to know about Andrew Kington is that he's a man who doesn't know how to lose.'

'A bit like Ben, then?' Caitlin said, unable to hide a shiver. 'If you could have seen the look in his eyes, Maggie, when he came round after Liam knocked him down . . . He wasn't just angry. It was way more than that. It was scary.'

'Andrew brought that child up to believe he was the Golden Boy, particularly after Jane, his mother, went back to the States. He thought there was nothing he couldn't do or have. But, unlike his father — who for all his faults worked his way up from nothing — Ben didn't work for it. He had everything handed to him on a plate, silver spoon and all, and he thought the world owed him.'

'Do you think I should tell the police about the fight?' Caitlin asked, the haunted look back in her eyes. 'I haven't told anyone except you. I don't know what to do.'

Maggie knew what a trauma it had been for Caitlin to give her account of the accident — she'd been the only witness — over and over again, each time leaving her more drained than the last. What was the point of putting the poor girl through all that again? Who would it help? Certainly not Joe and Andrew. And Ben and Liam were beyond help.

'But it wouldn't change anything, would it?' Maggie said gently as she put her hands over Caitlin's, surprised at how cold they were. 'All it will do is heap unhappiness on unhappiness; and God knows, sweetheart, there's more than enough of that around here.'

'I suppose you're right,' she said, but doubt still clouded her eyes.

'I know I am,' Maggie said firmly. It was time to steer the conversation back to Joe and Andrew. 'What do you know of your Mum and Dad's early days?' She picked up another smooth, round pebble and examined it carefully.

'I know Dad came to Stargate Bay when Mum was twenty-one and he was a couple of years older. Did you know him back then?'

Maggie nodded, her fingers working away at the pebble's smooth surface. 'Of course. Everyone knew everyone else in Stargate. That hasn't changed. Andrew was engaged to your mother at the time.'

'Andrew Kington and Mum?' Caitlin

stared at Maggie. 'My lovely, warm mother and that cold fish? No way.'

'Well, it's true. Andrew wasn't quite such a cold fish in those days — and he was a good catch. All the girls thought so. Plenty of money, even then; not bad-looking; fancy car. He had all the things that turn a young girl's head. Andrew and your mother had been going out together for a couple of years and planned to marry when Helen left university. But then Joe sailed into Stargate and everything changed.'

Maggie could still see the young Joe Mulryan that day as he brought the boat alongside the jetty with practised ease. The way his eyes danced with laughter when he threw Maggie the mooring rope and she missed it. And then there was his voice as he thanked her. It was as soft as Irish rain, and with a musical lilt that could make a shopping list sound like a poem. She had been captivated.

'Maggie?' Caitlin's voice brought her sharply back to the present.

'Sorry. Away with the fairies for a moment,' Maggie said gruffly. 'It happens at my age. Where was I?'

'Mum engaged to Andrew Kington.'

'Ah yes. Of course. Well, she was away at university when Joe first arrived, but she came home for the Christmas holidays; they met and, according to Joe, fell head over potatoes for each other. She broke things off with Andrew and married Joe instead.'

'But Andrew married someone else, didn't he? Ben's mother, obviously.'

Maggie nodded. 'He and Jane were married a week before your mum and dad. The biggest, flashiest wedding you can imagine, like he set out to show your mother what she was missing by marrying a penniless Irish boat-builder instead of him. Not that that cut any ice with your mother, of course.'

'And that's how the feud began? Because my mother chose my father instead of Andrew?'

'That was the start of it, certainly. Like I said just now, Andrew Kington doesn't know how to lose.'

'So what did he do?'

'He deliberately set out to cripple Joe financially. Then Joe got into serious debt buying the boat house.'

'Of course. Your father owned the boat house before Dad, didn't he? I keep forgetting that.'

I wish I could, Maggie thought bleakly. She swallowed hard and forced herself to go on with the story. 'My father was the reason Joe came to Stargate in the first place. He'd ordered this boat from Ireland for a customer, and Joe delivered it; he liked what he saw so much that he stayed.' She flushed and skillfully sent the pebble skimming across the water, this one going even further than the previous. 'Anyway, Joe mortgaged everything he had, and then some, to raise the cash to buy the business. But it left the pair of them constantly broke, particularly with two young mouths to feed. Which was why your mother went out to work. And then there was the car crash.'

'You're not saying Andrew blamed Dad for her death? Is that what this nonsense is all about? But Dad was nowhere near the car when she was killed. It was an accident, driving home from work in the fog. The inquest said so.'

Maggie shrugged. 'You know Andrew. He's never been one to let the truth stand in his way. He said your mum's car was poorly maintained by Joe, and that if he'd been any sort of man he'd have provided for his wife and family properly, and not forced her to work night shifts to pay the bills. He said that working nights to pay off Joe's debts had killed her.'

Caitlin's face whitened. 'How could he say that to a man who'd just lost his wife?'

Maggie hesitated. Had she said too much? She didn't want to make things worse, but it was too late now. She couldn't just leave things hanging.

'I'm afraid he did just that. It was the day before the funeral. Andrew came to the boat house, very calm, very matter-of-fact. He could have been calling in to discuss a repair job from the way he spoke. Only, of course, he wasn't. Instead, in that strange deadpan voice, he said how Helen's accident was all Joe's fault and that Joe'd robbed him of the woman he loved twice over. Poor Joe stood there without saying a word, nodding his head like he was agreeing with every word, even when Andrew said that if she'd never married him, she'd still be alive. Then, as if he hadn't said enough, Andrew went on . . . ' She stopped as she relived that terrible moment, as Joe stood there like a man who'd just been punched in the stomach.

'Go on,' Caitlin prompted.

'You know, lovey, sometimes things are best forgotten.'

'And sometimes, as you so rightly said just now, it's best to know the truth.'

Maggie sighed and prayed she was doing the right thing for Caitlin. 'As I said, Andrew didn't sound angry, which somehow only seemed to make it a whole lot worse. It wasn't something said in anger, in the heat of the moment, but something he'd planned and thought about. He just said, very quietly, that Joe had taken from him the one thing he loved and that he wouldn't rest until he'd taken everything from Joe.'

'Dad told you all this?'

A couple of hairpins tinkled onto the flat rock as Maggie shook her head. 'Well, no, not exactly. I happened to overhear them talking.'

Maggie knew very well there was a longstanding Mulryan family joke about the number of things she 'happened to overhear'. She didn't mind. In fact, she quite liked the way they teased her. Especially Liam, who had his father's laughing eyes and easy charm.

Only of course, there would be no more family jokes now. Not without Liam.

The long-threatened rain arrived in earnest. Caitlin called goodbye and ran down to the jetty to collect the dog, leaving Maggie sitting in the rain, wondering and worrying if she'd done the right thing.

Or whether it would have been better to have got the whole thing out in the open and put up with the consequences.

12

Nick looked up in surprise as Andrew came into the office. He was shocked by Andrew's appearance. He'd never had much flesh on him, but now the tailored grey suit he always wore to the office hung on him, and his narrow shoulders were more hunched than ever. His face was the colour of putty, and he looked like he hadn't slept or eaten in a week. Which, on reflection, Nick thought, he probably hadn't.

'I didn't expect to see you,' Nick said. 'And there was no need. Mrs Palmer and I are coping. Your business is in safe hands.'

'There's no point sitting around at home, staring at four walls . . . waiting for Ben to come through the front door, even though I know he never will.' Andrew's voice cracked and he cleared his throat. 'I'm better off working.

Besides, there are things I need to sort out about the funeral. People to invite. That sort of thing.'

'Of course.' Nick remembered the seemingly endless list of tasks involved in arranging a funeral only too vividly. 'Is there anything I can do to help?'

Andrew shook his head. 'I'll go through my contacts book with Mrs Palmer. She'll do the rest. There is one thing you can do for me, though, if you don't mind.'

'Name it.'

'Would you go and pick up Jane from Dorchester Station? She arrives on the 3.15. Oh yes, and she's staying at The Bull in Bridport.'

'Consider it done.'

Mrs Palmer had told him that Andrew and Jane Kington had divorced when Ben was six years old, and that she'd gone back to the States with a handsome divorce settlement in exchange for granting Andrew sole custody of Ben and the promise that she'd stay out of her son's life forever. A tough call. It was typical of the Andrew he was coming to know that he would not have his ex-wife staying in the house. Andrew Kington was, Nick was beginning to realise, a hard man to cross; and Nick looked forward to this contract finishing so that he could move on.

Nick knew better than most how a sudden bereavement could knock a person's whole life off the rails. He wondered how Jane Kington (or whatever her name was now) was dealing with the death of a son she hadn't seen in almost twenty years.

'Is she expecting me?' Nick asked.

'Who?' Andrew looked blank.

'Your wife. Is she — '

'My ex-wife,' Andrew snapped. 'And yes, she is expecting someone to collect her. You can't miss her. She'll have a pile of luggage a mile high. Jane never did get the concept of travelling light.'

* * *

Nick set off in good time, but a sudden storm swept the area and caused a number of minor accidents on the road between Stargate and Dorchester. He was ten minutes late when he finally pulled into the station car park. Jane Kington-as-was was easy to spot: elegant, perfectly groomed, and, as Andrew had predicted, surrounded by a mountain of luggage. She also had the saddest eyes Nick had ever seen.

'Mrs . . . Kington?' He made sure there was a slight pause between to words to give her chance to correct him. But to his surprise, she didn't.

'Yes, that's me. Andrew sent you, did he?'

'He did. I'm so sorry for your loss, Mrs Kington.'

'Thank you,' she said with quiet dignity.

As Nick began to collect her expensive matching luggage, he couldn't help remembering the last time he'd been in this station car park and the state poor Caitlin Mulryan had got herself into, struggling with her carrier bags of laundry. He almost smiled at the memory and wished, as everyone else must do, that he could turn the clock back to that time.

After polite enquiries about her journey, to which she gave brief but equally polite replies, she put her head back against the headrest and closed her eyes. The rest of the journey was made in silence, which suited Nick. He'd never been one for small talk, and it left him free to concentrate on driving through the rain, which was still coming down as hard as ever.

As they reached Bridport, he turned into the town's busy main street and pulled up outside the hotel. Jane gave a murmur of surprise. 'Oh, I thought . . .' she began.

'Andrew felt you would be more comfortable here.' Nick silently cursed his employer for putting him in this embarrassing situation. 'It's a great hotel. I've stayed here myself in the past.'

'I'm sure Andrew doesn't give a toss

for my comfort,' she said curtly. 'But thank you for the lift.'

As she went to get out, Nick stopped her. 'If you hang on, there's an umbrella in the back. I'll just get it.'

She shook her head. 'I haven't been away from England so long that I've forgotten what a bit of rain feels like,' she said.

She got out of the car, tilted her chin, and went into the hotel with Nick following her with the luggage. And he was pretty sure that the dampness on her cheeks was not caused by the rain.

13

'Archie. Come here, boy. You're getting soaked. Come here now, you daft dog.'

But Archie was not listening to me. Or if he was, he'd chosen to ignore me, so I had to go all the way out to the end of the jetty to fetch him. By the time I reached him the rain had plastered my hair to my head, and was trickling down my neck and soaking in to my T-shirt. I grabbed his collar and looked back through the curtain of rain to where Maggie was still sitting on the picnic rock. She was, no doubt, as wet as I was, and I wondered why she was still sitting there and not running for home.

I was having a hard job taking in what she'd just told me about Andrew, Dad and Mum. I still found it difficult to believe that Mum could have been engaged to him. As for those terrible things he'd said to Dad — no wonder there was such bad blood between them. What a shocking and cruel thing to say. And Ben and I had thought we could change all that. Or at least, I had. I'd been naive and stupid in more ways than one that night.

'Come on, Archie. We're both wet now. Let's go for a walk.' I figured a walk in the rain would lessen the chance of seeing anyone I knew. I still wasn't handling condolences very well and didn't know what to say to the well-meant expressions of sympathy. Besides, I've always been one of those weird people who enjoy walking in the rain — the stormier the better. 'We could both do with a bit of exercise and a change of scenery.'

I stopped off at the house to collect the dog's lead, change out of my wet clothes, and put on boots and waterproofs. Then I left a note for Dad, who was out goodness knew where again. Not that he'd notice whether I was there or not when he got back. But just in case.

The rain was coming down so hard, the house's shaky guttering had given up and the water cascaded down off the roof like a waterfall. The unmade lane outside the house looked more like a small river, and I noticed as I looked across to the beach that the storm had finally driven Maggie indoors; the picnic rock was now empty and the beach deserted, except for a couple of gulls scavenging among the seaweed on the tideline.

I headed for the cliff that rose sharply above the bay. The steep path that hugged the edges pulled at my calf muscles, and the sting of the rain on my face fitted my bleak mood perfectly. Thanks to the rain, there were no stunning views across the bay towards Portland to soothe me; no gentle waves lapping at the shore to beguile me. I couldn't even see the sea; only hear it pounding the rocks below.

Powerful enough to reduce rocks to pebbles. And boats to driftwood. Even boats as solid and well-built as *Storm Chaser*.

It was a mistake coming up here, high above the place where Ben and Liam had collided. How could I have been so stupid? I hardly needed reminding of the destructive force of the sea. So when I reached the top, I left the cliff path and instead took the bridle path that headed inland. The last section of the walk was down along the high-banked twisty lane that led back down into Stargate. At the sound of a vehicle carefully negotiating the narrow bends behind me, I shortened the dog's lead and stood in as close to the hedge as I could.

'Can I give you a lift?' It was Nick Thorne.

'No, thanks. My boots are muddy and the dog's dripping. Well, we're both dripping, as you can see. It's OK though. We can't get any wetter. I'm fine, honest.'

'This car's well used to muddy boots. I'll pull into that gateway down there and you can put the dog in the back.'

'No, really.' I didn't want to get into his car. Didn't want him to see how my face was burning as I remembered how Ben had warned me against him. Had that been another of Ben's lies? Along with the one about being in love with me?

'Caitlin?' Nick's voice, low with an edge of urgency, jerked me back to the present. 'I need to talk to you. And I'd sooner do it while we're on our own.'

I put the dog in the back, wiped as much of the mud off my boots as I could in the hedge, then climbed into the passenger seat.

He made no attempt to start the car but turned towards me, his face serious, his smoky grey-blue eyes troubled. 'It's about Liam.'

Liam? I'd psyched myself up to hear him say something about Ben. That he wanted to talk about Liam was unexpected, and my sense of unease intensified. 'What about him?'

'Did you know he'd gone for a job in

Poole the afternoon I gave you a lift home?'

I nodded. 'Of course I did. That's where he was when he should have been picking me up.' I remembered how angry I'd been with him that day and wished — oh, I'd wished a thousand times over since — that I hadn't. How insignificant it all seemed now. If only I'd known. I blinked hard and forced myself to speak normally. 'But how did you know?'

'Because I recommended him. The company's chief exec is a friend of mine. We were at uni together.'

'You recommended him? What for? And why?'

'They had a vacancy in their design department. And your brother has . . . ' He broke off. 'I'm sorry; he had great talent. He showed me his portfolio of designs and, whilst I don't know an awful lot about boats, even I could see he had something really special. That's why I recommended him to Alec.'

'Liam told me about the job.' His

dream job, he called it.' A stab of pain shot through me as I thought of all the dreams that would now never happen for him. 'He was so excited — but also concerned about how Dad would take it.'

'Did he tell Joe?'

I shook my head. 'He didn't get the chance. Dad went out soon after I got back and he was out again when I got up the next day. He'd taken the van for its MOT and came back — came back to find . . .' I swallowed hard. It didn't matter how many times I went over the events of that day; it never got any easier. How long would it take, I wondered, before I could think about it without dying a little inside each time?

'I'm so sorry,' he said softly. 'Your brother was a great guy. We had several drinks together.'

'You did?' Surprise made me speak without thinking. 'But Liam knew you were Andrew Kington's man. He'd never . . .'

'Maybe he didn't rate a stale old

family feud as importantly as you obviously do.'

'Oh, right. I see it all now,' I snapped, stung to recklessness by the sharpness in his voice. 'This was another of Andrew Kington's strategies to get at Dad, wasn't it? Take Liam out of the business with a job offer he couldn't refuse — and where would that leave Dad?'

I wrenched open the door, jumped out of the car, and stomped off up the road. But I hadn't got very far before he caught up with me.

'Now you're being paranoid and silly,' he said. 'The only ones who knew about the job offer were me and Liam — and Alec, of course. But that wasn't what I wanted to talk to you about. Get back in the car, please.'

'No, thank you.'

'Fair enough. Your choice. If you insist on us both getting soaked, that's fine by me. Just hear me out before you go marching off again. The reason I asked whether your dad knew about the job with Alec was because I know Liam had a load of papers relating to it. I went through them with him the day before. It occurred to me that if your father found them, it would be unnecessarily upsetting for him to learn that Liam was intending to leave him. There's no point in him knowing about it now, is there? I just wanted to warn you, that's all.'

'Oh. Right. Thanks,' I said, and wondered why this man always made me feel and act like a hysterical schoolgirl. I began to walk away, head down against the driving rain, horribly aware that I'd overreacted. But if he hadn't made that crack about me stoking up the old family feud . . .

'Caitlin?' he called after me, clearly not done.

'Don't tell me.' I whirled round, my eyes blazing, my voice heavy with sarcasm. 'Andrew Kington is Dad's mystery customer.'

He looked puzzled. 'I haven't the first idea what you're talking about. I was, in fact, going to ask what you want me to do with the dog. Only, he's in the back of my car, howling like he's sitting on a thistle. Shall I drop him at your house?'

I turned back. Poor Archie. He was standing up in the back of Nick's car, looking at me with worried eyes, his wet fur sticking up in little tufty spikes. How could I have forgotten the poor old chap? I still had his lead in my hand.

I thought I was going to laugh at the forlorn expression on his face. Instead I cried.

It had bothered me, ever since the accident, that I hadn't been able to cry. It was as if the shock of seeing Ben's boat spiralling into the air, then crashing down on Liam's, had frozen something inside me. But now, in the middle of the lane with the rain pouring down and the dog looking so pathetic, I was crying like I was never going to stop. I cried for Liam and Ben and young lives wasted. I cried for Dad and Andrew and all the broken dreams. I cried for poor old Archie, howling and forgotten, in the back of Nick's posh car.

Not to mention the odd few tears for the other really scary thing that freaked me out so much, I kept pushing it into that little compartment buried deep inside my mind marked 'to be thought about later'.

Deep, heaving sobs shook my body and I was powerless to stop them. I felt Nick's arms go round me, the warmth of his body as he held me close and, gradually, imperceptibly, the slight unravelling of the knot of tension that had lain coiled beneath my ribs for so long.

'I'm sorry,' I said eventually when there were no more tears. My eyes felt swollen and gritty, my throat like sandpaper. 'You're as wet as I am now.'

'It's fine.' He handed me a clean, dry tissue. 'I know what it's like to lose someone you love. I lost my wife eighteen months ago.'

I looked up at him and could see

from the pain in his eyes he was telling the truth.

'I'm so sorry.'

'It's a sad old cliché, which I know you won't appreciate at the moment — but time does heal, you know.'

'It's not just losing Liam,' I began, but stopped.

'It's OK. I understand. I saw you and Ben together that night.'

'You did? I didn't see you. When? Where?' My heart almost stopped. Had he seen us on the beach? I felt the colour creep up my cheeks and pressed the tissue to my face, hoping to cover it.

He grinned. 'You and Ben had eyes for no one else. I'm sorry. I wouldn't have asked you out if I'd known you and he were an item.'

How could I tell him that it wasn't grief for a lost lover that was eating me up, but the knowledge that I was responsible for the accident that had cost Liam and Ben their lives? How differently things might have turned out, for all of us, if Nick had been in the pub when I'd got there, rather than Ben.

If only. Who was it said they were the saddest words in the English language?

'I'd better go and see if I can find those papers,' I said. 'Thanks for telling me. If Dad finds them, it'll break his heart — and it's broken enough already.'

14

Thankfully, Dad was still out when I got home. I hurriedly dried the dog, then ran up the stairs to Liam's room. I hadn't been in there since the accident and had to take a deep, calming breath before opening the door.

It was a tip, as always. Like he'd leapt out of bed in a hurry, grabbed the nearest clothes and chucked them on, then rushed out. Just like he always did. What was different this time, of course, was that he wasn't going to come rushing back in, demanding to know what the hell I was doing messing about with his things.

I froze. I couldn't do this. Not today. My throat was still raw from crying all over Nick. I couldn't start again. Without Nick's comforting presence, I was afraid that this time I wouldn't be able to stop.

Liam and I were always squabbling. Dad used to say we were born having a go at each other. But he was my twin — and, most of the time at least, my best friend. A part of me that was gone forever. And things would never be the same again. I would have given everything I owned, and then some, to have him give me a hard time about nosing about in his room.

'Stop being such a girl and get on with it, Cait, for goodness sake.' I heard Liam's voice as plainly as if he was standing behind me. It jolted me into action.

I started to hunt around for the papers. Nick said when he'd last seen them they'd been in a blue folder with the logo of the company picked out in silver. But there was nothing remotely like that among the piles of boating magazines, junk mail and other rubbish that littered the floor by the side of Liam's unmade bed. I stretched out my hand to pull the duvet back on and straighten the pillows still dented with the imprint of his head from where he'd slept. But I couldn't do it. Not yet. I turned away from the bed and concentrated on the search.

The next obvious place to look was the back of the wardrobe where Liam always stashed things he didn't want me to find. Not that I ever told him I'd rumbled his very obvious hiding place years ago.

I opened the door and stood on tiptoe to search the top shelf. I thought I caught a glimpse of something blue and silver towards the back, poking out behind a haphazard pile of jumpers. I was about to reach for it when the door burst open.

'What the hell do you think you're doing?'

Dad stood in the doorway. White-faced. More furious than I have ever seen him.

'Come to paw over his things, have you?' he snarled in a voice that was scarcely recognisable. 'You just couldn't wait, could you now?'

'No. It wasn't like that,' I tried to say but he wasn't listening. He turned away and I screamed after him.

'Dad, for pity's sake. Don't walk away. Listen to me, will you? I . . . if you must know, I just came in here . . . to be a bit closer to him. That was all.'

He turned and came back into the room. It was like someone had burst a balloon as all the anger whooshed out of him. He looked old and ill as he sank down onto Liam's unmade bed, head bent, his large, capable hands resting, useless, on his knees.

'I'm sorry,' he whispered, his eyes shimmering with tears. 'I'm so sorry, sweetheart. It was just that as I came in . . . I came in and I heard movement in the room, and I thought . . . I thought . . . '

'You thought it was Liam,' I finished the sentence for him, the sick feeling back in the pit of my stomach. 'I'm sorry, Dad.'

I'm sorry I'm not Liam. Sorry you

think the wrong twin died, the stroppy ten-year-old inside my head screamed. But this time I held her in check. This wasn't about me.

'You're his twin, and twins are supposed to feel these things. Do you feel he's dead?' He tapped his chest. 'Here, inside?'

I turned away, not wanting him to see the rush of tears in my eyes. Andrew Kington was the lucky one. He had a son to bury, which would eventually give him some sort of closure. In spite of everything, Dad was obviously still clinging to a hope made all the more terrible since it was futile.

I'd been the only witness to the accident. I still saw it every time I closed my eyes. Every time I woke in the night, sweating and terrified. I saw Ben's boat rear into the air and crash down on Liam's. I saw the fireball that snaked across the water and engulfed them both.

'Dad,' I began tentatively, 'about tomorrow . . . '

'What about tomorrow?' he said tersely, all the softness gone from his voice now.

'It's Ben Kington's funeral. I'd like to go. Will you come with me? Please?'

His head shot up and his eyes blazed. 'Are you mad that you have to ask me that? You want me to go to the funeral of the man who killed my son?'

'I just thought . . . '

'And if I forbid you to go?'

'I'll go anyway.'

'Damn it, girl,' he snapped. 'Where's your sense of family loyalty?'

'It's this so-called family loyalty that got us into this mess in the first place,' I snapped back, as the sleepless nights caught up with me and a potent mixture of rage, grief and guilt boiled up inside me. 'I am going to Ben's funeral and you will not stop me.'

'For the love of Mike, do I have to spell it out? Andrew Kington will not be wanting a Mulryan at his son's funeral.'

'That's as may be. But — '

'And don't waste your tears on Ben.

He was a spoilt, arrogant, thoroughly unpleasant young man.'

Then I did something unforgivable. In amongst the grief for my brother, the guilt over my part in the row, the worry about my father, and the sadness for Ben and his family was this knot of anxiety that was getting harder to ignore with each passing day. It was like a switch had been flipped inside my head and it all came spilling out, whizzing and spitting like an out-of-control firework. Something that, until that moment, I hadn't even admitted to myself.

Sudden. Shocking. Shattering.

'I think I'm expecting Ben Kington's baby,' I said.

We stood on either side of Liam's untidy room. Both white-faced. Both shocked beyond words.

Had I just said that? For one crazy moment, I actually looked round. But there was no one else in the room, of course. Just me, Dad . . . and, maybe, Liam's ghost. Because I swear I heard him draw in his breath, laugh softly and murmur: 'Wow! Tell it like it is, why don't you, Cait?'

'I'm sorry, Dad. I didn't mean to tell you like that,' I said.

'And how were you planning to do it, young lady? With a fanfare of trumpets and a fountain of champagne?'

But before I could answer him there was a knock at the door. The sort of knock that would not be ignored. I looked out of the window, glad of the distraction. Until I saw what it was.

'Dad,' I said in a frightened whisper, 'there's a police car outside.'

15

After Nick dropped Caitlin and the dog off, he pulled into the little car park in front of the ramshackle old tearoom on the edge of the beach. It wasn't open, of course. Andrew said it was owned by 'a mad old bat', as he called her, who only opened when she felt like it, which wasn't often. Would she open more often when the new marina was built? he wondered. The new development certainly wouldn't do her business any harm.

He got out of the car and walked onto the beach. He needed to clear his head a bit before going back to the office. Caitlin's distress back there in the lane had stirred up a load of feelings best forgotten. For one crazy moment, he'd been tempted to tell her about Abbie. But it wouldn't have helped her, and it certainly wouldn't have helped him, so he was glad that he had, as always, pushed the memories away.

Trouble was, they wouldn't stay away. And now there was tomorrow's funeral to get through. He'd tried to get out of it, tried telling Andrew that he had no place there. But Andrew wouldn't hear of it. He'd insisted that Nick come, if only to look out for a number of business acquaintances that he knew would be there.

But the last funeral he had been to had been Abbie's. That had passed in a haze of misery and he remembered very little of it. But he knew the minute he stepped inside that church it would all come flooding back, and he didn't know if he was strong enough to cope with it.

Not just the grief. He was working through that, and he'd meant it when he told Caitlin that time does indeed heal. The racking pain had subsided to a dull ache and all the anniversaries had been got through, the birthdays,

Christmas, Mother's Day. He bent down and picked up a pebble and hurled it into the wind-whipped sea. Mother's Day! God, that had been a bad one.

The grief might be fading, but the guilt was as raw as ever. At least Caitlin Mulryan didn't have that burden on her slender shoulders.

As he turned to go, a police car drove slowly along the lane towards the Mulryans' house and boatyard. His heart contracted with pity. Did this mean that, at last, they'd found Liam's body? He hoped so. Maybe then Joe and Caitlin would have some sort of closure.

As he walked back to his car, the woman who owned the tearoom was just coming out of her house. She stood looking after the police car, her round face creased with worry. She hadn't seen Nick and was muttering quietly to herself. So she jumped as his footsteps scrunched on the gravel behind her.

'I'm sorry,' he said. 'I didn't mean to

startle you. And I hope you didn't mind me leaving my car there for a few minutes.'

'What? Oh, the car. No. Not at all. It doesn't matter a bit.' As she shook her head, Nick heard a hairpin fall to the ground. He bent down, picked it up and handed it to her. 'Oh, thank you. Very kind,' she said. 'You won't believe how many of those I get through in a week.'

She gave a half-smile, but Nick could see that her attention was only partly on him. Most of it was fixed on the policeman who was now getting out of the car.

'It's a sad business, isn't it?' he said softly.

'Tragic.' She looked at him as if seeing him for the first time. 'You're that young man who works for Andrew Kington, aren't you?'

'I am,' he said, half-expecting another tirade about being on the other side of the feud. But instead, her face softened and she looked at him closely.

'Poor Andrew. How is he coping?' she asked.

'Better than . . . ' He was about to say 'better than I did when I lost my wife', but checked himself. What was that all about? This wasn't about him and Abbie. *See what happens when you let the demons out? They dominate your every thought, ambush you when you least expect it.* But there was something about this woman — a million miles away from the mad old bat Andrew had described — that invited confidences.

'He's coping better than I'd have expected,' he said, and moved towards his car.

'The funeral's at eleven tomorrow, isn't it?' she called after him.

'That's right.'

'I'll see you there then,' she said.

As he drove off, he noticed that she still hadn't moved. Her eyes were fixed on the police car, which had now stopped outside Joe Mulryan's house. Something about the expression on her face told Nick this wasn't mere nosiness, but a genuine and deep concern for her neighbours.

He wished he'd had a neighbour like that, looking out for him.

16

The dog and I both jumped up at the sound of the front door opening. Archie gave a gusty sigh when he realised it wasn't Liam, and went back to sleep. I tensed as I waited for Dad to come into the kitchen. It was nearly an hour since he'd left with the policeman to have a look at some wreckage they'd found. Forty-eight minutes, to be precise.

It's a weird, geeky thing I do, but when I'm stressed I count. Forty-eight minutes. Two thousand, eight hundred and eighty seconds. I know that because I'd counted every single one of them while my mood swung from fury that Dad had refused to let me go with him, to black despair.

Maggie came knocking on the door within minutes of Dad driving off, but I hadn't answered and hoped she'd assume I'd gone with Dad. Like I should have done, only he hadn't wanted me to. He'd told me to stay in such a way that I wasn't sure if he was talking to me or Archie.

But my anger, which had been bubbling away for every single one of those two thousand, eight hundred and eighty seconds evaporated at the sight of him. He hadn't shaved for several days and he had the beginnings of a white, whiskery beard. There were deep lines around his mouth that I hadn't noticed before. And his shoulders were hunched. For the first time in his life, he looked like an old man.

'Was — was it . . . ?' The question stuck on my tongue.

'It was *Storm Chaser*,' he said heavily. 'At least, part of it. The top of the cabin, which must have sheared off on impact. There was no sign of Liam.'

No sign of Liam. I hadn't realised until that moment that I'd been holding my breath — had probably been holding it for the entire forty-eight minutes. Now it came out in a long, shaky sigh. But whether it was a sigh of relief that Liam's body wasn't in the wreckage, or a sigh of despair that for us the agony of waiting went on, I didn't know.

'Where was it found?' I asked.

'Just half a mile south of Cadbourne Beach.' He shook his head. 'It must have come in on this morning's tide. I checked it out yesterday afternoon.'

Cadbourne Beach is part of a designated nature reserve and one of the most deserted stretches of the entire Dorset coast. Its high, steeply shelved pebble banks are usually only used by a few hell-bent fishermen who refuse to be put off by the long, calf-blistering trudge along the shingle to get there. It's surrounded by marshland and is not exactly the sort of place you'd take Grandma and the kids for a game of rounders and a picnic.

'Is that where you've been going every day?' I asked. 'Why didn't you tell me?'

'Not just Cadbourne. Up and down

the coast. Although given the currents and the tides, Cadbourne was the most obvious. I thought there might be more wreckage washed up, though. I thought . . . ' He sat down heavily and dragged a weary hand across his face, his fingers rasping across the whiskery stubble. 'Sweet Mary and Joseph, I could murder a drink, so I could.'

'I'll make you some tea.'

'Tea won't do it. I'm having a whiskey. Will you be having one?'

'No, thanks.' The thought of any sort of alcohol, not just Dad's favoured Irish whiskey, made my stomach churn.

He poured himself a large one and took a long pull at it, then sat down opposite me, his expression grave. 'I think it's time to finish that little discussion we were having before the law interrupted us, don't you?' he said quietly while my already queasy stomach gave another uncomfortable lurch. 'I didn't even know you and Ben Kington were involved.'

How could I explain my relationship

with Ben to him? If I told him the truth, that Ben had made a fool of me and boasted about it to Liam, how would that help? And yet, I didn't want Dad to think I was the sort of girl who went in for one-night stands.

'We weren't exactly involved,' I began, then went on quickly as his head shot up, his eyes frowning, 'What I mean is, it was early days. We were . . .' My voice trailed away under his fierce gaze. 'We — I didn't mean it to happen,' I finished lamely.

'You don't mean he forced himself on you, do you?' he said, anger lighting up his eyes. 'Because if so — '

'Of course he didn't. It was nothing like that. It was the night I came home from uni. You'd stormed off — Liam too — and I was at a loose end and he was very nice to me. Bought me a few drinks, and . . . well, you know.' My voice trailed away and I couldn't look at him anymore. Not when he was looking at me like I was something that had been stuck to the bottom of his shoe.

What I'd felt for Ben hadn't been love. I could see that now. It had been no more than a girlish crush that had become a sort of habit I'd never grown out of. I'd never seen the real Ben, the one Dad and Liam saw — spoilt, arrogant, and selfish.

What happened between us on the beach shouldn't have. And it certainly shouldn't have resulted in a baby. A new life should begin in an act of mutual love and commitment, not in a haze of vodka-fuelled recklessness. And yet, for a few short hours, I thought we'd found something in each other that until then neither of us had been aware of. Surely he'd felt it too? It couldn't all have been down to the alcohol and the heat of the moment — could it?

'I meant to go into town the next day and get the morning-after pill,' I said. 'But then Liam and Ben had this fight . . . ' I stopped, hand over my mouth. I hadn't meant to tell him. But it was too late.

'A fight?' His eyes bored into mine. 'You didn't say anything about a fight. What were they fighting over?'

When I didn't answer he reached across and grabbed my wrist, tight enough to make me wince. 'It was you, wasn't it? They were fighting over you.'

Miserably, I nodded my head.

'Go on,' he ordered. 'Tell me.'

So I did. I told him how Liam had hit Ben, got into *Storm Chaser* and roared off, and how Ben had come round and taken off after him, swearing to get back at him. Even though I felt desperately ashamed and couldn't face looking at Dad, it was a relief to finally tell him.

He let go of my wrist, got up and stared out the window. 'Have you told anyone this?' he asked without turning round.

'No,' I said, rubbing my wrist. 'Well, only Maggie. I asked her if I should tell the police but she said not to. That it wouldn't help anyone, just cause a lot more upset. Besides, I didn't want

Liam's memory to be . . . well, you know.'

'And did you tell Maggie about . . . about your . . . situation?' He was looking, not at me, but down at the label on the bottle, staring intently at it as if he were committing every word to memory.

'Do you mean the baby?' He nodded. 'No. I haven't told anyone. Except you. I thought . . . '

He took another gulp of whiskey as my voice petered out. 'Well, you did the right thing there, girl, if nothing else.' He turned back to me, his voice now brisk. 'Now, I don't know how you go about this sort of thing. You'd best make an appointment with the doctor. He'll sort it.'

'Sort what?'

'The abortion, of course. The sooner it's done, the better.'

'No.' Instinctively my hand went to my stomach.

The look of surprise on his face would, at any other time, have been funny. I was always the compliant twin — the one always trying to win his approval, always wanting to do what he wanted, be what he wanted. But not this time.

'What the devil do you mean?' he demanded.

'I mean, I am not having an abortion.' I sounded a lot more composed than I felt. I didn't want a baby. Of course I didn't. And I certainly didn't want Ben Kington's baby. So why had I just said that?

Yet as soon as Dad started calmly talking about abortion, like it was no more than a handy way of tidying away a minor inconvenience, I knew I couldn't go through with it.

'Don't be ridiculous, Caitlin. You can't throw away everything you've worked for because of some drunken fling with a man who'd run away from you faster than a rat up a drainpipe if he was still alive.'

'I'm not throwing anything away,' I said firmly. 'I don't care what you say,

Dad. I'm having this baby.'

'Then how about I say this, girl?' He leaned towards me, his eyes glittering. 'And believe me, because I mean every word. If you go ahead with this baby, then you will have to leave this house. Because I will not have Ben Kington's — '

'Don't you dare say that word,' I cut in before he could say it.

With calm deliberation he placed his glass on the table. The room was silent except for the ticking of the clock and little whooping sounds as Archie hunted rabbits in his sleep.

'I mean it, Caitlin.' His quiet, carefully controlled voice was a million times more frightening than his previous anger. 'I knew in my bones that Ben Kington was to blame for Liam's — for Liam's accident. And what you've just told me confirms that. Either you get rid of his — his child, or you are no longer welcome in this house. It's that simple.'

'For pity's sake, Dad.' Panic spiralled

up inside me as I tried to ease the tension with a small forced laugh. 'This isn't the nineteenth century. I'd never have had you down for a 'don't darken my doors' kind of guy. Come on, it's not even snowing outside.'

But there was no answering smile. 'You leave me no choice,' he said coldly. 'I'm sorry.'

'Sorry? Yes, of course you are.' My chair clattered unheeded to the floor as I pushed myself away from the table. 'Just like you're sorry the wrong twin died.'

17

'Caitlin. Come along in.' Maggie's smile of welcome vanished as she saw the expression on my face. 'Oh Lord, is it Liam? Have they . . . ?'

I shook my head. 'Some wreckage from *Storm Chaser* turned up. Dad went down to identify it. But there was no sign of Liam.'

Her kitchen looked as it always did — as if Hurricane Harriet had just blown through. I dropped my rucksack on the floor and sank into the big, squashy armchair, breathing in the familiar and comforting scents of baking: cinnamon, chocolate and vanilla.

'You going somewhere?' she asked, looking at my rucksack.

'I'm going to find a B and B. Just for a couple of nights. Dad and I have been getting on each other's nerves a bit and we need to give each other space.'

Space? That was one way of putting it, I thought. I should have answered the questions I could see in Maggie's kind eyes, but a wave of tiredness washed over me and I sank back in the chair. 'I just called in to ask you to . . . to keep an eye on him, will you? And to make sure he remembers to feed Archie.'

'Don't take too much notice, lovey. Joe always did have a hasty tongue,' she said. 'And with the grief and worry, he's not himself.'

'Isn't that the truth? Did you know he's been going out every day, up and down the coast, looking for Liam?'

'Poor Joe.' She switched the kettle on, peering out of the window that overlooked the bay as she did so. 'But there aren't many men around here who know the coastline better.'

'But what if he finds him?' This was what had gone through my mind when he told me. And even though I was cross with him and hurt beyond words by what he'd said, I still worried about him. 'How will he cope if he's on his own? It would be awful, wouldn't it? I wish he'd leave the search to the police and coastguard. I offered to go with him, but that was before . . . ' I felt my throat start to close over and got to my feet. 'I'd better go.'

'You're going nowhere, except to my spare room. Here, take this.' She passed me a cup of tea and a slice of Dorset apple cake big enough to feed an entire under-tens football team.

'I'll take you up on the room, thanks, but pass on the cake, if you don't mind.' I looked down at the soft, buttery cake studded with caramelised apple and encrusted with crisp brown sugar, and my stomach gave an uneasy lurch. 'I'm not hungry.'

'Stay and drink your tea, then, while I go up and get it ready.' She picked up my rucksack and bustled out before I could change my mind.

* * *

Maggie's heart was thudding as she hurried up the stairs. But it wasn't the stairs making her heart race, although she was really going to have to do something about her weight one of these days. It was the thought of what, if anything, she was going to say to Joe. She didn't know what he and Caitlin had fallen out about and she didn't want to know. It was none of her business, as Joe would be only too quick to point out, no doubt. But surely the man could see his daughter was going through hell at the moment, without him adding to it? Then again, maybe it was just as Caitlin said — maybe the pair of them just needed a bit of space. Should she say something, or leave well alone?

She paused at the entrance to her spare room as a thought occurred to her. In all the years she'd lived in this house, she'd never had anyone to stay. Never had any reason to.

Her father had owned the little two-bedroom cottage on the beach forever, but had let it out as a holiday cottage for years. They'd moved in after he'd sold the boatyard and house to Joe. She'd hated living there at the time; hated being so close to Joe and Helen, and wanted to get as far away as she could from them. But then her father became ill, so she stayed. Then after her father died, her mother became ill, and suddenly it was too late. It was never the right time to move on, and she'd been here ever since. After her mother died, she'd moved her things into their bedroom, and since then nobody had slept in the little single bed that used to be hers in the room that overlooked the bay.

She collected clean bed linen from the airing cupboard, then went into the room and straight across to the desk by the window. She peeled the yellow Post-it notes off the laptop screen and closed the lid. Then she gathered up some papers and put them in the drawer. Out of habit, she looked, as she always did when she came in here, along the lane to Joe's house. What had they rowed about that was so bad it had forced Caitlin to pack her bag? Had the girl told Joe about the fight between Ben and Liam? Had the prickly old fool blamed Caitlin for it? Her lips compressed. She'd have words with Joe Mulryan if that were the case. This whole situation was getting out of hand.

She stripped off the old blanket that usually covered the bed and put the clean pillowcases, sheet and duvet cover on as quickly as possible. Anxiously, she tested the mattress. Would it still be as comfortable after all these years? She should have done something about replacing it ages ago, but there had never seemed any point.

Would Caitlin be OK here? The poor girl looked as if she hadn't slept for a week. And as for her refusing the apple cake . . . it was one of her favourites, second only to chocolate cake. Maggie's heart ached for her and she wished she could do something — anything — to banish that sad, empty look from her eyes.

She took one last look at the bookcase. There wasn't time to clear everything out. She'd just have to hope Caitlin didn't notice. Or, that if she did, she wouldn't make the connection.

And then there was the desk by the window that gave her a perfect, uninterrupted view of Joe's house and yard. What would she make of that?

18

It seemed an age before Maggie came back, and I really hoped she hadn't gone to too much trouble. To be honest, I'd have been happy to sleep in the squishy armchair in the kitchen.

But in spite of my tiredness, I was intrigued as she showed me up to the room. I'd known Maggie all my life and had been in and out of her house on a regular basis, but only ever on the ground floor. Liam and I had been banned from going upstairs, and we would often speculate on what she kept up there that she didn't want us to see. Liam thought it was smuggled goods, her house being right on the beach; but I favoured a mad relative locked in the attic, as I'd been going through a *Jane Eyre* stage at the time. Now I realised she was simply a person who valued her privacy, and I felt quite guilty at the prospect of invading it. At the same time, however, I was very grateful — and, if I'm honest, more than a tad curious.

The small white-walled bedroom was almost monastic in its simplicity, with just a single bed, a small white cupboard, and a bookcase. The only other piece of furniture was a plain wooden desk and chair in the alcove of the bow window.

'Wow. Isn't that something?' I leaned on the window sill and looked out at the view I'd known and loved all my life. I'd always been fascinated by the way it perpetually changed; no two days were ever alike, as the colour of the sea reflected the sky. Today, the sun left sparkling flecks of gold on a turquoise sea; a marked contrast to yesterday's dark, angry storm clouds.

'This is your room, surely? It's got to be the best view in the house. I can't let you give it up.'

'Believe me, you're not. My bedroom's at the back. The sea would keep me awake otherwise. No, I come in here and do a bit of writing sometimes, that's all.' Maggie pointed to the desk, which held nothing but a laptop, a jar of pens, and a notebook. Its neatness was in stark contrast to her comfortably chaotic kitchen.

'I didn't know you wrote, Maggie.' I was intrigued. 'What sorts of things?'

'Oh, it's just a bit of scribbling. It'll be nothing you've ever read, I'll bet.'

She looked so embarrassed that I let the matter drop. 'The room looks very comfortable. It also has the added bonus of being perfectly placed to look out for Dad.'

Maggie nodded and looked even more uncomfortable. 'Yes, I suppose it has. Although I hope you don't think I spend all my time spying on you and your family.'

'Of course not. You've been such a good friend to us over the years, the way you've looked out for us all.'

'That's what neighbours do,' she said.

'And you and Dad have been friends forever, haven't you?'

'We've known each other a long time, yes. Ever since he came to Stargate, in fact.'

There was something about the way she spoke — a softness in her voice that was echoed in her eyes. And then I remembered the way she'd coloured up that time she told me about how Dad and Mum had met. Surely, she didn't mean . . . ?

'You and Dad?' Of course. It had to be. How could I have been so blind?

She didn't need to speak. I could see the answer in the blush that began at her neck and spread across her face. 'It was all a long time ago,' she mumbled.

'So you were the reason Dad stayed on in Stargate after he delivered the boat. Were the two of you an item?'

'An item? Do you mean, were we going out? That's what we called it back then. Yes, we were for a while.'

A thought suddenly occurred to me. 'So were you and Dad engaged? As well as Mum and Andrew?'

'No. No. Well, not officially. But we had what I suppose you could call an understanding.' She picked a pen out of the pot on the desk and twirled it around in her fingers. 'My parents were delighted. Joe worked in the boatyard with Dad, you see, and Dad thought the world of him. So when Joe and I talked about getting married, Dad sold him the boatyard but said he was in no hurry to be paid, now Joe was more or less family.'

She looked so upset that I put my hand on her arm. 'Maggie. It's OK. You don't have to say any more.'

'Yes, I do,' she said firmly. 'It was all a long time ago now. And, looking back on it, my parents really pushed us together. Poor Joe didn't have time to draw breath. My father was already quite ill at the time, and I think he saw Joe as a way of safeguarding the business and settling my future — and Mum's too, of course. He had it all planned. But then your mother came home for the Christmas holidays, she and Joe met, and that was it.'

'Head over potatoes?'

'Exactly. Dad was that hurt and angry with Joe, so upset on my behalf that he insisted on being paid back immediately for the boatyard. And that, I'm afraid, was the beginning of Joe's money troubles.' She put the pen back in the pot and looked up at me, her eyes troubled. 'You see, your dad borrowed some money, not realising that it was from a loan company owned by Andrew Kington. As soon as that happened, it was like he'd popped his head inside a noose. Andrew had him exactly where he wanted him and could tighten the noose any time he pleased. Which he did. Over the years he tightened it again and again, and is still doing so. Exorbitant interest rates. Joe couldn't get credit, and was blacklisted by his suppliers. His money problems just went on and on. And Andrew was behind them all.'

'And that's been going on all these

years? Still?' I thought of the heavies that Ben had sent round the day before my graduation, remembering too the way he'd boasted of it to Liam. My heart ached, and the last of the resentment I felt towards my father melted away. 'Poor Dad. That's shocking.'

She nodded. 'It's something I still feel very bad about. If only I'd made my father stop and think about what he was doing. He wasn't a hard man, just very upset on my behalf — and, of course, the end of his plans. But I should have talked him out of it. He died before the consequences of his actions became apparent. He'd be horrified if he could see how it all turned out. I feel kind of responsible.'

'Well you shouldn't.' I reached out and touched her hand. 'This is all down to Andrew. The man really is a monster, isn't he?'

Maggie gave a wan smile. 'Like I said, he doesn't know how to lose.'

'And this was what he meant when

he said he'd take everything from Dad?'

'It seems like it. Poor Joe. Because now, of course, he has. The business, and now his son. Thank goodness he still has you.'

But he doesn't want me. The words flashed into my head but I didn't say them aloud. I'd said too much already. 'Was that why you never married, Maggie?' I said, changing the subject to something more comfortable. For me at least. 'Was it because of Dad?'

'No, not really. As I said, my father was ill when Joe first arrived, and he died not long after Joe and your mum married. Then there was my mother. She was very frail and never got over Dad's death. I couldn't leave her, could I?' She gave a wobbly smile. 'All water under the bridge now, lovey.'

Isn't it weird how you can know someone for as long as I've known Maggie, and then find out you never really knew them at all? I decided to tell her at least part of what Dad and I had rowed about.

'I told him I was going to Ben's funeral and he said I wasn't to go. This wretched feud seems so stupid and pointless, especially now. I understand a bit more now about what went on between Dad and Andrew, and it's pretty bad. But this should never have carried over to the next generation.'

Maggie sighed. 'You're absolutely right, of course. You know, I saw you and Ben go past that night. You looked so good together, and I thought how brilliant it would be if you and he got serious about each other and could eventually end the rift between Joe and Andrew. Were you very much in love with him?'

I gave a short laugh to cover the way my heart almost leapt out of my mouth. She'd seen me and Ben together? Had she guessed how our stroll along the beach had ended?

'I thought I was. But as for seeing us as a present-day Romeo and Juliet, I'll remind you that the original story, like ours, ended in tragedy. The sort of happy-ever-after ending you describe only happens in romantic novels.' I stopped myself from making a snippy comment about romantic novels as I noticed for the first time that the bookcase was full of them. Maggie was obviously a huge fan. 'Not that I've anything against romance,' I added quickly.

'Help yourself to any of them.' She saw my glance at the bookcase. 'And don't you go worrying about that old fool of a father of yours. He'll come round. Once Ben's funeral is over, maybe things will be better.'

'Not for me and Dad,' I said shortly.

'Look, I've got to go out for a bit. Will you be all right here?'

'Of course. I need a bit of time to sit and think. I'll be fine.'

Only, I wasn't fine. As soon as the door closed behind Maggie, I realised that sitting and thinking was the last thing I needed, as my mind began trundling down the old familiar spiral of regrets and recriminations. Looking for a distraction, I crossed to the bookcase and gave a start as one of the titles leapt out at me.

It was *Storm Chaser*.

Intrigued by the coincidence, I picked up the book and began to read. Within minutes I was drawn into a fast-paced, exciting story that was as far from my previously held opinion of romantic novels as you could get. I curled up on the bed and was soon transported to another world, far away from my own troubles. Pure escapism. Exactly what I needed.

* * *

Maggie didn't even bother knocking, as she knew that if Joe saw it was her, he wouldn't let her in. She'd come prepared with the key he'd given her for emergencies. And this, as far as Maggie was concerned, was an emergency. Joe Mulryan was going to get a much-needed piece of her mind.

She'd always felt bad about her

father's part in Joe's troubles, and it was a relief to be able to tell Caitlin about it finally. She'd half-expected her to be angry, but she wasn't. Just sad.

Joe was in the kitchen, Archie in his basket by the cooker. Archie looked up as Maggie came in and gave a half-hearted flick of his tail, but Joe didn't move.

The sight of him sitting there with his head in his hands, a half-empty bottle of whiskey in front of him, almost weakened Maggie's resolve. He'd always been a fighter. Even when Helen had died, he'd come through it fighting; bewildered, lost and grieving, but determined to make a life for his two young children.

But not now. Now he looked broken. And Maggie didn't think she, or anyone else, could mend him.

'Joe?' she said quietly. 'Joe, look at me.'

He looked up at her and the last of her anger evaporated. She sat down opposite him and took his hand in hers.

'I've just come to tell you that Caitlin is with me,' she said.

'Caitlin.' He pulled his hand away and reached for the glass but she got there before him and moved it out of his reach.

'You said some pretty hurtful things to her, Joe.'

'She said some pretty hurtful things to me,' he said with a flash of his old spirit. 'Did she tell you?'

'She blames herself for Liam's death, Joe. It's eating her up inside. Not only that, but she thinks you do, too.'

He looked bewildered. 'Why should she think that? I never blamed her, not for a moment. The only person to blame for Liam's death was Ben Kington. And then she calmly tells me that she's expecting his baby.'

Caitlin was pregnant? The shock must have shown on her face because Joe gave a short laugh.

'Yes. It's a shocker, isn't it? My daughter and Ben Kington. How did she think I was going to react? Hardly likely to break out the champagne, am I?'

'Maybe not.' Maggie was still trying to take it in. 'But throwing her out isn't the answer either.'

'I didn't throw her out. I gave her a choice. Get rid of the baby or get out. Simple as that.'

'Oh, nice one, Joe. That's a big help. For pity's sake, man, think about it for a minute.' Her voice softened as she attempted to get through to him. 'The poor girl must be in turmoil. She's just lost her twin brother, and the man she loved, and now she finds she's pregnant. She could do with a bit of support right now, not censure.'

'It's none of your damn business, and I'll not be lectured in my own home. Get out.'

Maggie had reached the end of her patience. 'Shame on you, Joe Mulryan,' she snapped as she pushed her chair back. 'I dread to think what Helen would say.'

'Leave her out of it,' he growled.

'And shut the door on your way out.'

'Don't worry. I'm going. And Caitlin will be staying with me until you come to your senses and apologise.'

'Me, apologise? I'll not — '

'That's all I have to say, Joe.' She pushed the glass back towards him. 'I'll leave you to your whiskey. And don't forget to feed the dog, will you?'

19

I was so caught up in the *Storm Chaser* story, I was quite startled when Maggie tapped on my door to say goodnight.

'Is that the time? I'm enjoying this book so much, I completely lost track. It's a cracking story, isn't it? Beautifully written and utterly unputdownable, if that's a word.' I marked my place carefully and looked at the cover. 'Why haven't I heard of this author before, Maggie? You could have told me. You're obviously a great fan, as you have a load of her books.'

'She has her moments,' she said grudgingly, which was so unlike her. She was usually full of enthusiasm for something she'd read, and eager to pass it on to me. To my surprise I saw she was embarrassed, as if she was taking the praise personally.

And then, finally, I made the

connection. The laptop, the workman-like desk, the bookcase full of books all by the same author. How slow on the uptake was I?

'Oh God, Maggie. It's you, isn't it? You're Margot Astlebury. All these books.' It explained something that had always puzzled me and Liam. How on earth, when she only opened the tearoom when she felt like it, had Maggie been supporting herself all these years? Looking at the number of books in her bookcase finally solved the mystery. 'You wrote these, didn't you? How many are there?'

'Over forty now. I've been writing them for years.'

'But they're brilliant. Certainly this one is. I can't wait to read the others.'

She bit her lip, her eyes anxious. 'You won't tell anyone, will you, Caitlin? I wouldn't want it to get about.'

'But whyever not? I'd be so proud if I'd written something half as good as this.'

'But there's something faintly ridiculous about a fat old spinster like me, with a face like a pickled walnut and a figure like the before picture in a slimming advert, writing trashy novels about love and romance.'

'That's nonsense,' I said hotly. 'You're none of those things. And your writing is anything but trashy. It's brilliant.'

She smiled. 'Well, thanks for that. I'm glad you're enjoying it.'

Later that night, as I was drifting off to sleep in Maggie's extremely comfortable spare bed, something else occurred to me. The book I was reading was called *Storm Chaser*. Was it a coincidence that the boat Dad had built was also called *Storm Chaser*? And hadn't Liam said something about the mystery customer insisting on the boat's name?

So, could it be that Maggie was Dad's mystery customer? I tackled her about it the next morning, as she was preparing breakfast.

'You're the customer who insisted the

boat be called *Storm Chaser*, aren't you? The title of your first novel, according to the blurb on the back.'

'Would you like bacon and eggs?'

I shook my head as a wave of nausea washed over me. By the time it had passed, Maggie had placed a rack of toast in front of me.

'Best you eat something,' she said. 'I've read that dried toast helps.'

I flushed. 'Sorry. I seem to have picked up a bug. I hope I've not passed it on to you.'

'I doubt if what you've got is infectious, lovey,' she said with a smile which faded as she leaned across, patted my hand and said something which made me completely forget she hadn't answered my question about *Storm Chaser*'s mystery buyer. 'The baby's Ben's, isn't it?' she went on softly. 'That's what you and Joe were fighting about, wasn't it?'

I nodded and took a bite of the toast. It felt like brick dust in my mouth.

'Are you going to tell Andrew

Kington?' Maggie asked.

'I haven't even thought about that. But I don't see him being any more thrilled with the situation than Dad was. As for the idea that the baby could bring the two of them together, I'm afraid that sort of happy ending would only happen in one of your books, Maggie, not in real life.'

She sighed. 'More's the pity. That's the beauty of writing books, you know. I think it's what got me writing in the first place. When the world you live in seems to be spinning out of control, it's great to be able to escape into a world that you *can* control. Where you get to decide the outcome.'

'Maybe I should try it,' I said with a laugh.

'Maybe you should.' She smiled. 'At least you're looking a bit better now. Surprising what a good night's sleep will do.'

'Not to mention a good book,' I added.

'Well, I would say that, wouldn't I?'

Her face became serious again. 'Now, lovey, would you like me to come with you to the funeral today? I was going to go anyway, and we'd be company for each other.'

A surge of relief washed over me and I gave her a grateful, if somewhat tremulous, smile. 'I'd like that very much. Needless to say, Dad won't be there.'

But at least I would have someone to hold my hand as I prepared myself to say a silent goodbye to the man who, whatever else he was, was the father of my unborn child.

20

Nick pulled up outside Jane Kington's hotel a few minutes early; but even so, she was waiting for him in the reception area, a tall elegant figure in black, her bright blonde hair coiled at the nape of her neck, in striking contrast to the dark clothes.

'Andrew called to say you'd be collecting me,' she said. 'Thank you for that.'

'You're welcome. Did you sleep well?' he asked politely.

'I never sleep well.' She said it as a statement of fact rather than an appeal for sympathy. Then she turned her head to stare out of the window, making it very clear that she wanted no more small talk. Nick understood and sympathised. Neither did he.

The village of Stargate was in two parts. There was Lower Stargate which consisted solely of the beach, a few houses, The Sailor's Return and Joe Mulryan's boatyard. Most of the rest of the houses were to be found about half a mile further up the narrow, twisty lane in Higher Stargate. The tiny grey church stood right in the middle; and by the time Nick reached there, the lane was already choked with cars. Clusters of people were gathered around in the churchyard, quietly chatting before going inside.

He parked the car, then got out to open the door for Jane. Having done so, he turned away to get back in the car.

'Aren't you going in?' she asked.

He held her gaze for a moment. 'No,' he said quietly. He had no intention of sitting through the service, although he'd promised Andrew he'd be around afterwards. 'I don't do funerals. But I'll be around here after the service and will go back to the house, so I can give you a lift if you need one.'

'That won't be necessary, thank you,'

she said coolly. 'Thank you, too, for collecting me.'

Nick stood by the car and watched as she walked along the path that wound among the lichen-crusted gravestones, the stone paving slabs worn smooth by centuries of footsteps. He saw her look towards someone she obviously recognised and check her stride as if to greet them. But before she could do so, the woman turned her back quite deliberately and walked away. Nick saw a quick flush stain Jane's cheeks. Then she squared her shoulders and walked through the now-silent groups toward the church. She looked so in control. So dignified. But so alone.

On an impulse he locked the car, walked quickly through the churchyard and caught her up just as she went in. Whatever demons were waiting for him, Jane obviously had a few of her own as well. He didn't want her to face them alone.

She was the boy's mother, for goodness sake, yet she chose to sit near the back. Nick slipped into the pew beside her. She gave him a small, tight smile, her eyebrows slightly raised, as she picked up an order of service. He heard her sharp intake of breath as she turned it over and saw a picture of Ben printed on the back. It had obviously been taken on a boat; his face was tanned, his shock of blond hair whipped by the wind, his eyes dancing. He looked excited and happy — and full of life.

Nick looked quickly down at his own order of service. He didn't want her to know that he'd seen how her hands shook and her lips pressed together. She was very like Ben; or rather, he supposed, Ben was very like her. Same poker-straight blond hair, same wide-apart blue eyes.

Suddenly the organ wheezed into life and the coffin, borne on the shoulders of four of Ben's mates from the rugby club, swayed slowly down the aisle. As it got closer to them, the scent of lilies filled the church. Lilies. Of all the flowers to choose. Abbie had carried lilies in her wedding bouquet, and their scent always reminded Nick of that day and how beautiful she looked.

Powerless to stop them, the memories surged back. He was no longer in the tiny grey church looking down on Stargate Bay, but in the large, golden-stone parish church in the small Yorkshire town where he and Abbie had lived all their lives. The church where they had got married. And where Abbie and their baby daughter were buried.

Now, instead of the overpowering fragrance of Ben's lilies, he could smell the delicate scent from the simple spray of sweet peas, Abbie's favourites, that had been on her coffin. He could see the sad-faced vicar who'd known and loved Abbie all her life. He could hear Abbie's favourite hymn, 'Lord of the Dance', even though everyone in Stargate church was singing 'All Things Bright and Beautiful' for Ben.

He wanted to get up and run away. His first instinct to stay away had been right. This was the reason he didn't do funerals.

* * *

I watched the sunlight as it streamed in through the stained-glass windows, making little splashes of colour on the ancient oak pews and lighting up a brass plaque commemorating a family whose line went back centuries but ended, as did so many, with the First World War. It always made me sad to read the inscription, but today it was more poignant than ever. Their 'dearly loved son' was even younger than Ben and Liam when he lost his life in the war that was supposed to end all wars.

As we took our places at the back of the crowded church, Maggie touched my arm and pointed to a blonde woman in black sitting two rows in front of us. 'Jane,' she whispered.

Ben's mother. I remembered how she'd left Stargate one summer, the year Mum died, supposedly going back to the States on a visit to her family, but never returned. There had been talk about her having an affair, but all anyone really knew was that she and Andrew were divorced not long after and she hadn't seen him or Ben since.

Liam reckoned it was easier for Ben, seeing as his mother was still alive. But I always thought it must be harder to deal with the fact that your mother chose not to be with you. What made a woman walk away from her child like that? Ben was only about twelve at the time. I could understand her walking away from her husband, but her child? It didn't make sense.

And how strange it must be for her, at the funeral of the grown-up son she'd never known. She wasn't even sitting near the front. OK, so she probably wouldn't have wanted to sit next to Andrew, any more than he'd have wanted her to do so. But right at the back? It was very sad. And it hadn't gone unnoticed by many of the local people there, judging from the number of heads turned in her direction, the raised eyebrows, the whispered comments.

As the coffin swayed slowly down the aisle, the scent from white lilies on the top filled the church and added to the sense of unreality. I simply couldn't associate Ben with those flowers. I looked down at the Order of Service, at his photograph on the back: leaning in towards the camera, laughing, his eyes sparkling — unlike the last time I'd seen him, when those same eyes had been blazing with hatred. I shivered and tried to remember instead the man I'd been with in the Sailor's that night, who'd made me laugh, who'd sat on the beach with me and counted the stars. Surely it hadn't all been a lie, had it?

My thoughts slid away from Ben and moved, as always, to Liam. How soon would it be before we would be going through all this for him? One thing I vowed: he was not going to have white lilies on his coffin. I'd go out along the cliff path and make him a wreath of wind-twisted hawthorn and spiky yellow gorse.

The longing for my stupid, annoying, desperately loved twin, the other half of me that would now always be missing, was unbearable.

Most of the service passed in a haze of misery for me and I longed to get away, to go home and take Archie for a walk along the beach where I could say goodbye to Ben — and Liam, too — properly. As we left the church, blinking in the strong sunlight, Maggie looked at me anxiously.

'Are you all right, lovey?' she said. And her sympathy was nearly my undoing.

I shivered as a seagull wheeled overhead, its mournful cry reminding me of Liam's theory about the souls of the dead. Like I needed reminding.

'I just need to get away. Be on my own for a bit.'

'I understand. Are you all right walking back?'

I nodded. 'The walk will do me good.'

'OK, if you're sure. Then I'll go and have a word with Jane Kington,' she murmured. 'The poor soul. You'd think she had leprosy, the way everyone is avoiding her.'

I began to walk away. Before I could do so, however, someone called my name. With barely concealed impatience, I turned back to see Nick coming towards me, unfamiliar in a charcoal-grey suit, white shirt and black tie.

'Yes?' I said and for a moment he looked at me blankly, like he couldn't think who I was or what he wanted me for. 'You wanted me?' I prompted.

'Oh, yes. Yes. Sorry, I'm a bit . . . ' He dragged his fingers through his thick dark hair, looking a million miles from the cool, in-control guy who'd threaded his big car through the busy main-road traffic that day we first met. Back in what now seemed another lifetime. 'I . . . oh yes, that's it. I wanted to ask, did you manage to find the folder before your father did?' he asked.

Now it was my turn to do the staring blankly bit.

'The folder. About the job Liam went for?' he went on. 'I talked to you about it yesterday.'

Was it only yesterday he'd given me a lift in the rain and warned me about getting rid of the folder that would prove Liam was planning to leave before Dad found it?

'Oh yes. Thanks for reminding me. I found it. But before I could do anything about it, something . . . something else came up.'

The pain must have shown on my face. 'I heard they found some of the wreckage,' he said softly. 'That's tough.'

I nodded. 'Dad's still looking. Still hoping . . . ' I blinked hard and looked down at my feet. There was no way I was going to cry all over him again.

'Andrew's asked me to say everyone is welcome back at the house,' he said.

I shook my head. 'I don't imagine

that invitation was meant to include me.'

'Oh Caitlin. Caitlin.' He repeated my name like he was a frazzled schoolmaster and I the rather dense pupil. 'You're not still playing that idiotic Kington versus Mulryan game, are you? Don't you think it's time to let it go?'

I bristled at the unfairness of it and spoke without thinking. 'Believe me, Mr Thorne — ' My voice was icy, my use of his surname deliberate. ' — no one would like to see an end to that particular game, as you call it, more than me. I ended up the loser, big time, if you remember. I lost my brother and . . . ' I checked myself in time. I'd been going to say 'and the father of my baby'. How daft was that? 'And Ben,' I finished lamely, shaken by what I'd so nearly blurted out.

His face went from irritation to contrition in an instant. 'I'm so very sorry.' He touched me briefly on the arm, his eyes anxious. 'That was a stupidly insensitive thing to say. Forgive me. It's just that . . . ' He paused, then shrugged. 'I have no excuse, only to say that it's been a difficult couple of days.'

Like they've been a walk in the park for me, I was about to say with a flash of irritation. Only I didn't. Because when I looked closely at him, I could see he was genuinely upset. In fact, he was more than upset. He looked like a man who'd been to hell and back. Was he really that fond of Ben Kington? But then I remembered how yesterday he'd said something about losing his wife, and my heart went out to him. The funeral service had obviously brought it all back, poor guy.

I took a step towards him, my hand outstretched. I wanted to put my arms around him, to hold him close the way he'd held me yesterday and tell him everything was going to be all right. To say something, anything, to banish that awful bleakness from his eyes. Only the sound of a car engine starting up somewhere behind made me stop and think about what I was doing. Of the shocked embarrassment on his face had I done so. That was the trouble with funerals. They jangled up the emotions and made you say and do the weirdest things.

'For heaven's sake, you don't have to apologise.' I gave him my warmest smile. 'Funerals have that effect on me as well.'

'So, will you come?' he asked. 'I assure you, Andrew won't care one way or another.'

I looked up as the car, the whisper-quiet, the mirror-like finish of its black paintwork gleaming, the chrome sparkling in the sunlight, glided slowly past. Inside was just Andrew and an elderly couple I assumed were his parents. But no Jane, of course.

I thought of Dad, out there in his old van somewhere, driving up and down the coast every day searching in vain for the wreckage of the boat. I thought of Archie, sitting on the end of the jetty every day waiting for Liam to come home. I thought of Andrew Kington, a lonely figure in a great big car; and of Jane Kington, sitting at the back of the church at her son's funeral. Lastly, I thought of the picture of Ben I still held in my hand: laughing, happy, full of life. What a waste. A stupid, terrible waste.

'No, I won't, if you don't mind,' I said gently. 'And it's nothing to do with family feuds, I promise. I just need a bit of time on my own.'

But as I walked away, Nick's phone rang. After a brief pause, he called me back. 'No, it's OK,' I heard him say. 'I'll tell her.'

'Tell me what?' The way he looked at me as he spoke made me feel something cold and hairy was crawling up my back.

'That was the police,' he said. 'They've had my contact number since the accident. They've been trying to get in touch with you or your dad but couldn't raise either of you.'

'Dad never has his phone on,' I said, suddenly feeling the need to talk fast and non-stop. All I could think of in that brain-freeze moment was that I needed to stop him saying anything else. Because whatever it was, judging by the look on his face, it was something I didn't want to hear. 'But mine — of course, I turned it off before the service like you're supposed to do and forgot to turn it back on again. Which, I realise now, was very silly of me, because of course you never know, do you, when you might . . . '

'Caitlin,' he cut across my demented chatter, like he knew why I was gabbling. He took both my hands in his and the sympathy in those grey-blue eyes freaked me out. 'I'm afraid they've found the rest of the wreckage of *Storm Chaser*. This time there's no doubt. I'm sorry.'

It felt like the air had been sucked out of my body. 'And . . . Liam?' I forced myself to ask.

'There's no sign of him yet, but they're sending the divers down,' he said gently. 'Except . . . '

'Go on.'

'They found a distinctive gold chain caught up in part of the wreckage. The sort you used to find on old-fashioned pocket watches. They wondered if you or your father might be able to identify it.'

After Mum died, Dad had given Liam and me the chain that used to be on her father's pocket watch. He'd had them made into matching bracelets for us and we both wore them all the time.

Sunlight glinted on the heavy gold chain that encircled my outstretched wrist. 'I can do better than that,' I whispered. 'I can show them the other half.'

At least Dad hadn't been the one to find the rest of the wreckage of *Storm Chaser*. For that, if nothing else, I was thankful.

21

Nick stepped closer as Caitlin swayed slightly, her face chalky white. For a moment he thought she was going to keel over and was getting ready to catch her.

'Would you like to sit down over there for a moment?' He pointed to a nearby bench in the shade of a yew tree, well away from the people who were still thronging the small churchyard.

She still looked shaken, but her voice was steady as she said, 'No, thanks. I just need to get home.'

'How did you get here? Did you drive?'

'I . . . ' For a moment, she looked as if she was having trouble remembering, but she appeared to collect herself. 'No. I came with Maggie. She drove.'

'Is that the woman who runs the

tearoom in Stargate?' Nick asked. 'The one over there talking to Jane Kington?' He was relieved to see that someone, at least, was talking to Jane, and that she looked slightly less strained than she had earlier.

'Yes, that's Maggie. But I don't want to drag her away. It's OK. I'll walk.'

'No. I'll take you.' He put his hand under her elbow, led her towards his car and opened the door for her. 'Sit there for a moment while I tell Jane.'

'Nick?' she called him back. 'Don't tell Maggie — about Liam. She'll want to come with me and I . . . I really do need to be on my own for a bit.'

Maggie did indeed want to go to Caitlin, but Nick suggested that she take Jane to Andrew's house instead.

'But I wasn't going to go,' Jane said.

'I think you should,' Maggie said, then turned to Nick. 'I'll go with her, if you're sure Caitlin's all right.'

He wasn't sure Caitlin was all right, but he didn't tell Maggie that. He hoped that Joe was back home by now, but as the car bumped along the rough track towards the Mulryan house, it was obvious that he wasn't.

'Would you like me to stay with you until your father gets back?' he asked as he pulled up outside the house. She shook her head and got out. He got out too and walked up the path behind her.

'It's all right. I'm fine, honestly.' She looked far from fine, but she had that look in her eyes that dared him to question it. It was the same look Abbie used to get sometimes — that 'I know what I'm doing' look — when it was perfectly obvious she didn't.

'It's no trouble. I'll just hang around for a bit,' he said.

'No.' Her refusal was sharp and he could see the effort it cost her to soften her tone. 'No, thank you. Dad will be back soon, I'm sure. And besides, I really, really need to be on my own for a while.'

'Would you like me to come to the police station with you?' he asked, unable to walk away from her in spite of her assurances.

She shook her head. 'No, you get back to Andrew. I'll wait for Dad and we'll go together. That's how it should be. Thank you, Nick. For everything. I really appreciate it.'

For a brief, mad moment, he had an almost overwhelming urge to pull her into his arms and hold her like he would never let her go. The intensity of the feeling shook him and he felt quite ashamed, coming as it did so soon after reliving Abbie's funeral with such intensity. He whispered a silent apology to his dead wife, got back in his car and headed back to the church.

But he wanted to stay so badly it hurt.

* * *

I closed the door behind Nick, relieved to be on my own at last. For a moment there, I thought he was going to refuse to go. But I think he realised that I was saying nothing but the truth when I said I wanted — needed — to be on my own, if only to work out how on earth I was going to tell Dad. It was kind of Nick to offer to go to the police station with me, but that was something Dad and I had to do together.

I sat down at the kitchen table, put my head in my hands and tried to think. Archie came up to me and put his head in my lap. I fondled his silky ears. 'There's no more going out to sit on the end of the jetty for you, boy,' I told him. 'No more Dad sailing up and down the coastline either. But how am I going to tell him, eh? It's going to break his heart. I'll just have to be strong for both of us.'

Archie gave a big gusty sigh, like he understood every word; although in fact what he was probably doing was enjoying having his ears rubbed and thinking that I didn't do it as well as Liam used to.

I was still trying to work out how best to tell Dad when I heard the wheezing rattle of his old van pulling up outside. I went to the door to let him in but before I could say anything, he pulled me into his arms and hugged me so hard I could scarcely breathe. My face was pressed against his soft, fleecy jacket which smelt, as always, of the sea, engine oil, and those peppermints he always carried.

'Darling girl, I'm so very sorry. I behaved like a total idiot yesterday. I was awake all night, thinking of what you said — you know, about how the wrong twin died. But you couldn't be more wrong, sweetheart. If at times it felt like I favoured Liam over you, that's only because Liam and I are — were — so alike.' He loosened his hold and smoothed back a lock of hair that had fallen across my eyes. 'You, on the other hand, get more like your mother every day. And sometimes, even after all these years, it gives me a real jolt, so it does. Right here.' He tapped his heart.

'It's OK, Dad. I never really believed it,' I assured him. 'It was just one of those stupid heat-of-the-moment things. But, the thing is — '

'The thing is, sweetheart, it was just like history repeating itself. All I could think of was how much your mother wanted to be a teacher when we first got together; how we'd worked out how we could afford it so that she could go off and do her teacher training. But how before she could take her place, she got pregnant with you and Liam. I didn't want you to make the same mistake.'

At any other time I would have teased him about calling me and Liam a mistake. I could even have reminded him that Mum had told us this story many, many times but had always said that she'd never for a second regretted her lost chance.

But not this time. Instead, all I could do was wonder how on earth I was going to tell him.

'I was so relieved when Maggie came by to say you were with her,' he went on. 'And to give me a right old ear-bashing as well. Well deserved, of course.'

'Dad, please.' As gently as I could, I eased myself away from him. 'Sit down. I've got some news.'

Finally, he read the expression on my face, heard the flat tone of my voice, and slumped into the chair. He looked like I'd just taken him out at the knees.

'They've found Liam?' His voice was barely above a whisper.

'They've found the rest of the wreckage. And . . . ' I swallowed hard and held out my wrist. ' . . . and the other half of this. You know Liam would never take it off. It must have . . . during the explosion . . . '

I couldn't go on. I couldn't think anymore of Ben's black and scarlet boat, engine screaming, crashing down on *Storm Chaser*; of splintering debris showering into the air before being engulfed by the fireball. Of the gold chain ripped from Liam's wrist by the blast. Of Liam . . . my infuriating, maddening, beloved brother.

As I'd sat there waiting for Dad to come home, I'd promised myself I'd be strong for him. Instead, it was him comforting me, rocking me in his arms the way he did when I used to have nightmares, in those first bleak months after Mum was killed.

'Hush now,' he said after a while. 'You'll do yourself harm, sweetheart, going on like that. And you have the baby to think about now. We both do.'

I caught my breath. Did that mean . . . ?

'You're . . . OK? About the baby?' I said between short hiccupy breaths.

'Well now, I'll admit it wasn't what I'd have planned for you. But whatever you decide, I'll be here for you.' He brushed aside my halting attempt to thank him. 'Come along now. Let's have a drink before we go down to the police station. And this time, we'll both have tea.'

I'd just picked up the teapot when the dog started barking. I froze as Dad and I looked at each other, our faces mirroring the same shock.

Archie wasn't doing the warning barks he did for the postman and strangers, but the ecstatic, yodelling frenzy he reserved solely for . . .

'*Liam!*'

22

I don't know which one of us said his name. It could even have been both of us. All I knew was that Liam stood framed in the doorway, staggering slightly under Archie's over-the-top welcome: bruised, unshaven, and wearing strange baggy clothes that I'd never seen him in before. But definitely Liam.

'Get down, you fool,' I yelled at the dog who took no notice, as usual. But Archie ignoring me was the only usual or normal thing going on at that moment.

How do you feel? Have you noticed that's what journalists ask at times of great stress, or excitement? *How do you feel?* If someone had stuck a microphone under my nose right then, my answer would have been pure gibberish. Would have made no sense. Because I was feeling almost every emotion in the book. A kaleidoscope of sensations was flashing through my head like flickering fast-frame pictures.

First came disbelief. I was going out of my mind and seeing what I wanted to see. Then suspicion. Obviously I was asleep and would wake up any moment. After that, clusters of impossible-to-name emotions, jangling and tangling around inside my head like tights in a tumble dryer. As for Dad, he'd stood up and was grasping the back of a chair as if it was a lifebelt and he'd just jumped off the *Titanic*.

Later came joy, anger, relief, fury — every possible feeling you could think of, and then some. None of which I could have found the words for at the time, no matter how many microphones were stuck in my face.

Then I said the daftest thing. But I had the teapot in my hand and my brain had frozen. I doubt if I could have told anyone my name at that moment.

'We were just going to have a cup of tea.' I sounded like I was inviting the vicar in for cucumber sandwiches on the lawn. 'Would you like one?'

Daft it may have been, but it had the effect of ending the paralysis that had affected everyone in the room — except of course the dog, who was still capering around, trying to get Liam to notice him. Dad crumpled into his chair like he'd been cut off at the knees, Liam let go of the carrier bag he'd been holding and, if the rolling pin had been handy, I'd have probably whacked him around his poor bruised face with it.

Instead, I dropped the teapot, wrapped my arms around him and hugged him, saying his name over and over. I pulled back, though, as I heard his quick intake of breath.

'What is it? Are you hurt? Oh my God, Liam. I thought . . . we *all* thought . . . you were dead. I saw the explosion, the boats shattering, the fireball . . .'

'That was Ben's.' Liam turned to Dad. 'You built *Storm Chaser* well, Dad. You always said that hull would withstand anything — and so it did. It saved my life.'

'What happened? Where have you been?' Dad sounded as shocked and messed up as me.

'I've got to sit down.' Liam eased himself into a chair, wincing as he did so. 'Seriously, Cait, if your offer of tea still stands, I'd love one.'

'You're hurt,' I said. 'What's wrong with you?'

'Concussion and three broken ribs, but all on the mend now.' Archie rested his head on Liam's knee and went into doggy ecstasy as Liam fondled his ears in the way that only Liam could. 'I don't remember much about the accident. Just this loud crack, a blinding flash, then nothing.'

'Nothing at all?' I said, a hundred questions flooding my mind. 'But how . . . ?'

'Give me time, Cait. I haven't got it sorted in my head yet. There are still gaps, particularly the accident. It's all fragmented. Like I was floating in and out of a dream. I remember one time, it was almost dark. The boat — or what was left of her — was drifting. The cabin roof was gone, and there was a damn great hole where the engine mounting was. I couldn't move, and was in such pain I thought that was it: curtains. I must have slipped in and out of consciousness throughout the night.'

I stared at him. 'You mean, you just sailed away after the accident?'

'Not sailed away. Carried by the tide.'

'But I was there on the jetty when it happened. I can't believe I didn't see *Storm Chaser* go clear.'

Liam looked puzzled. 'Weird. Didn't anyone else see it?'

'No. I was the only witness. But I didn't have my phone, so I ran off to get help. If only I'd stayed, I'd have seen you. But I thought . . . '

'You did the right thing, Caitlin. You went to get help,' Dad said firmly. 'Go on with your story, Liam. It's still not making a lot of sense to me.'

'When I came to properly, it was

daylight. I realised the pain in my back came from a broken stanchion that had fallen across me. Once I'd managed to wriggle free, I could see I was being carried towards Cadbourne Beach.'

'I knew that was where the current would have taken you,' Dad said. 'But I've trudged up and down every last inch of it, turned every damn pebble. How come I didn't find you?'

Liam looked down at his hands and muttered so quietly neither of us heard him.

'What did you say?' I prompted.

'I said, you didn't find me because I didn't want to be found.' His voice was only slightly clearer and he looked down at Archie, not at us. 'I'm so, so sorry. You both must have gone through hell and back. But I was in a blind panic — I wasn't thinking straight. All I could think was that I'd killed Ben and wrecked your boat. I wanted to run away and keep running. So I waited until the current took me within swimming distance of the beach, then jumped in and swam for it.'

'And the boat?' Dad asked.

'I scuppered it. I didn't want it washed up on Cadbourne Beach, sparking off a search. It's out there in the bay. I can take you to it if you like.'

'You don't have to. It was found this morning,' Dad said. 'Caitlin and I were about to go down to the police station and identify it.'

Liam's face paled, accentuating the livid purple and yellow bruises that ran down one side of his face. 'I'm so sorry for what I've put you through. But like I said, I was panicking. I really thought I'd killed Ben back in the boat house. I landed him a punch and he went down, cracking his head open as he fell.'

'It was the corner of the workbench,' I said, reliving the moment.

'The blood,' he said with a shudder as he, too, relived it. 'I thought he was dead; that I'd killed him. Nobody would believe it was an accident. I didn't mean to hit him that hard.'

'But if you thought you'd killed him,

who the devil did you think was in the boat that crashed into you?' Dad thundered while Archie whined and pressed closer to Liam.

'I thought it was Andrew. I only got a glimpse as he was closing in on me. I thought he'd come to blow me out of the water for killing his son.' Liam's hand shook as he passed it across his poor, bruised face. 'He drove straight at me like a madman. I've never been so scared in my life.'

'But you didn't kill Ben,' I said. 'He died in the crash.'

'I know that now. I saw it in the paper and realised that.'

'That was nearly two weeks ago, boy. Where have you been since then?' Dad looked so angry I thought he'd have a heart attack. I placed a calming hand on his arm, but he swatted it away like an annoying fly.

'Let him finish, Dad,' I said.

Liam flashed me a grateful smile. 'I swam to the beach, and spun a fisherman a yarn about getting caught out by the tide and that I'd been knocked about a bit after a fall on the rocks. He took me back to his motorhome in the car park and gave me a hot meal and a change of clothes. He was a really nice guy. He wanted to take me to hospital, but I refused. Then he said he was heading off down the coast towards Weymouth, so I asked him to drop me off. I've got a mate down there. Remember Danny from school?'

'Drop-out Danny?' Of course I remembered him. He'd dropped out of everything — school, work, anything that resembled a conventional way of life — and ended up living with a group of Travellers on a patch of waste ground just outside Weymouth.

Liam nodded. 'Danny took me to A&E, got me patched up, then let me crash in his caravan. He said I was well out of it for a few days.'

Then Dad asked the question I'd been dying to ask. 'Why didn't you contact us; let us know you were OK? You must have realised we'd have assumed the worst.'

'It never occurred to me you'd think I'd died in the accident.' Liam sighed. 'I figured someone would have seen *Storm Chaser* heading off and assumed I'd done a runner, so it would be best if you didn't know where I was. You've got to understand, I was really scared. I thought I'd killed Ben. I'd brought such shame and worry on you both, I figured you'd be better off without me. I picked up the phone several times, but the longer I left it the harder it got.'

'So what finally changed?' I asked.

'Danny came back yesterday with some fish wrapped in last week's copy of the local paper, and there was the whole story about Ben's inquest, the accident and everything. So I hitched a lift . . . and here I am. I'm sorry. Really, really sorry.'

Dad's chair screeched on the floor as he stood up, his eyes blazing, his hands balled into fists. 'Sorry? You think that's enough? You think all you had to do was turn up, ask for a cup of tea, and say you're sorry? Have you any idea what you've put your sister and me through?'

'I know. And I'm sorry.'

'You can say sorry until you're blue in the face, but I'll never forgive you for this, Liam. Never.'

He got as far as the door when something inside me erupted. 'Dad! Get back here this minute,' I yelled, 'and sit down.'

He looked as if he was about to protest, but I pointed to the chair. 'No, I mean it. Sit down. Both of you.'

And he did. As did Liam. The two of them sat at either end of the kitchen table, while Archie slunk into his basket. The sight of the three of them watching me anxiously would have had me collapsing in giggles at any other time. But not this time. This was way too serious.

'Our lives have been blighted by people who can't forgive and forget — and that includes you, Dad,' I went on. 'And Andrew Kington. Maybe if the two of you hadn't brought your sons up to carry on your stupid vendetta, Ben would still be alive. And Liam wouldn't have spent the last couple of weeks scared witless, thinking he'd killed him.'

'This is different,' Dad said. 'Liam — '

'I did what I always do when things get tough,' Liam said shamefacedly. 'I legged it. But no more. I'm going to tell the police, about the fight and everything.'

'But why?' I said. 'You landed a lucky punch, although maybe an unlucky punch would be a better way of describing it. Ben went down and hit his head on the workbench. But it was a very superficial cut and looked a lot worse than it actually was. It was his pride that was hurt, that was all. But when he came round, Liam, I was really scared for you. I've never seen anyone so out of control. He took off like a bat out of hell after you, and was so wound up I think he rammed you quite deliberately, without thinking of the consequences.'

'He was coming straight at me, that

was for sure,' Liam said. 'I tried to turn the boat, but I wasn't quick enough.'

'Look, nobody knows about the fight except me and Dad. Oh yes, and Maggie. They all think what happened was simply a tragic accident. The inquest said so. So why don't we leave it like that? For the sake of Ben's memory.' I thought of Andrew Kington's drawn face. 'Don't you think Andrew's suffered enough? Does he really need to know that it was caused by Ben's recklessness and out-of-control temper?'

Dad nodded. Liam looked from him to me and back to him again. His eyes were unnaturally bright as he drew a long, shaky breath. 'There's something else I have to tell you, Dad,' he said, and for the first time, he was looking Dad in the face.

'Liam, no,' I tried to stop him, figuring Dad had had enough shocks for one day, but Liam held up his hand.

'Let me finish, Cait. I need to do this.' He took a breath. 'The thing is,

Dad, the day I should have picked up Caitlin from the station, I was on my way to Poole for a job interview.'

'A job interview?' Dad echoed. 'Doing what?'

'On the design team of a firm of boat builders in Poole. They offered me the job there and then. Although whether they will now, of course . . . ' He shrugged.

'And when were you thinking of telling me?' Dad asked, his voice cold, his eyes fierce.

'I know, Dad. I should have told you I wanted out of the business — and I was trying to, honest. But you put such a store on me taking over, and with things going so badly and everything . . . ' His voice petered out and for a few moments there was silence, save only for the ticking of the kitchen clock and the distant sound of the waves breaking on the beach outside.

Nobody moved. I stared at Liam. Liam stared at Dad. Dad stared out of the window. It was as if we'd all frozen again, like we had when Liam had first reappeared. This time it was Dad who broke the silence.

'I'm taking the dog out,' he said, shrugging on his fleece. 'I need to do some thinking. Don't either of you do anything or go anywhere until I come back. Especially you, Liam. Understood? Come along, Archie.'

Archie gave Liam a soulful look, like he couldn't bear to be out of his sight, even to go for a walk. But Dad clipped on his lead and the dog followed reluctantly.

Liam let out a long, shaky breath as the door closed behind Dad and Archie. 'Jeez. I've made a right mess of things, haven't I?'

He wasn't wrong there, and I was about to tell him so when I realised that the horrible grey blanket of misery that had pressed down on my shoulders for the last couple of weeks had gone.

Liam — my infuriating, exasperating, best mate of a brother — was alive. Nothing else mattered.

23

Nick's mind was still very much on Caitlin as he drove towards Andrew's house. He'd hated leaving her, but understood her need to be alone. He'd been very much the same after Abbie died. As he was negotiating the narrow lane out of Stargate, he met Joe coming down. Nick reversed back into the gateway for him and received a curt nod of thanks for his pains. At least now they could make that trip to the police station together.

When he reached Andrew's house there were still little knots of people standing around, talking in undertones, taking surreptitious glances at their watches to see when they could politely leave. He looked across at Andrew, talking to the vicar who'd taken the service. Andrew looked strained and ill, and Nick could well appreciate the huge effort it was taking him to hold things together.

Why do we put ourselves through this? he wondered. *Why stand around in your own home making small talk, when all the time you just want to shut yourself away in an empty room and howl at the moon?* At least, that was what he'd wanted to do at Abbie's wake; not stand and listen to a load of people trotting out all the clichés about time being a great healer and how life goes on. On and on and on. Until he wanted to scream at them to go away and leave him alone.

And yet, of course, they were right — up to a point. His life was going on, and the pain was no longer so raw; but he still had times when he wanted to howl at the moon.

He stared out of the window, forcing himself back to the present by focusing on the magnificent view. A huge floor-to-ceiling mullioned window looked down across the bay, where the sea was a rich turquoise and the cliffs were gilded a deep ochre by the afternoon sun. He wondered, though, what pleasure it gave Andrew now, knowing that his son was killed out there, and how soon it would be until he sold this lovely old house.

'It's a grand view, isn't it?' a voice said softly behind him. 'The best in the area.'

He turned round to see Caitlin's friend, Maggie, standing behind him. 'Is Caitlin all right?' she went on, her eyes full of concern.

'She was a bit upset,' he said. 'Hardly surprising. But I passed Joe in the lane, so he'll be with her now.'

Maggie sighed. 'Poor girl. This sorry business has hit her hard. As for Andrew, he looks like he's aged ten years in the last couple of weeks. It must be the worst thing of all to lose a child. They say it's something you never get over.'

'Excuse me,' Nick said, his voice more curt than he'd intended. He was on the point of walking out, of getting into his car and driving somewhere — anywhere, it didn't matter — when he saw Jane Kington. She was standing alone by the big oak-panelled fireplace. Her face was pale and drawn, and there were deep shadows under her eyes.

'Are you all right?' he asked her. 'You look all in.'

She gave a bleak smile. 'It's the jet lag catching up with me.'

'Would you like a lift back to your hotel?'

'That would be great, thank you,' she said. 'Maggie very kindly offered, but it's too far out of her way, and I was about to call a cab.'

Nick was only too glad to get away. 'I'll just go and tell Andrew we're leaving.' He crossed the room, catching Andrew's eye as he drew near.

'I'm taking Mrs Kington back to her hotel,' he said. 'She says the jet lag's caught up with her.'

Andrew looked across at Jane. For a moment Nick thought he was going to say something to her. Instead, he nodded and turned away. Nick pretended not to notice the way her eyes suddenly welled up at the cold dismissal.

'My car's a little way down the road,' he said when he reached Jane's side once more. 'That was as close as I could get. Would you like to stay here while I fetch it?'

'No.' Her reply was swift. 'I mean, thanks, but the walk will do me good.'

They drove, as always, in silence, until Nick glanced across at her, alerted by a small sound. She was crying, the tears slipping silently down her cheeks.

'Do you want me to stop the car for a bit?' he asked.

She shook her head but he stopped anyway, pulling into a lay-by near the entrance to a park. They were just minutes away from the street where the hotel was, and he reckoned she needed time to compose herself. Come to that, so did he.

He'd almost lost it back there with Maggie and hadn't meant to be so rude to her, something he regretted now. She was only trying to be kind and, of course, she couldn't have known how her well-meaning words had hit home. It was indeed a terrible thing to lose a child.

Jane's voice suddenly broke into his bleak thoughts. 'There was no one else,' she said. 'Everyone thought I'd had an affair and that Andrew had thrown me out. But it wasn't like that at all. I loved Andrew, but it's hard knowing that your husband loves someone else. And when Helen died, things were even worse. He made no attempt to hide his feelings for her. I couldn't compete with a ghost, that was for sure. So I went back home to see my folks and sent Andrew one of those stupid 'it's me or her' letters, you know what I mean? To my horror, he wrote back saying our marriage was a mistake, that he was very sorry but he'd never loved me, and that he would not contest the divorce but would give me a very generous settlement and would send my things on. Which he did. It was such a shock.'

'Mrs Kington, you don't have to explain.'

'But I do. I've seen the way people have looked at me today, judging me. How could she abandon her son? That sort of thing. And I want to put the record straight, but not for my sake. Why should I care what people around here think of me? It was for Andrew's sake.'

It was as if she'd been bottling up these words for years, and now they came tumbling out and she was powerless to stop them. 'You see, it wasn't Andrew who kept me from seeing Ben,' she went on. 'I know that's what people think, but it's simply not true. It was Ben. When I told him I wouldn't be coming back to England; that my life was in the States now — I didn't tell him that his father had virtually thrown me out — he said he hated the States and that if I didn't come back to his father, he'd have nothing more to do with me.'

'He was hurt and angry, surely. Lashing out the way kids do,' Nick murmured. 'It's a pretty normal reaction.'

'That's what I thought at first — that he'd get over it in time. But he never did. Instead, he cut me clean out of his life. Birthday cards and presents were returned unopened, phone calls refused, emails deleted. I tried everything. Andrew tried as well, to give him due credit. But Ben would not be swayed. You see, Nick, he couldn't bear not to get his own way. Not in anything.'

Nick was at a loss to know what to say. He hadn't known Ben Kington very long, but it was long enough to know that his mother's summation of his character was probably an accurate one. 'That's tough. What will you do now?'

She shrugged. 'Go back to the States, I suppose.'

'I notice you still call yourself Jane Kington. Does that mean you never remarried?'

'Yes. Believe it or not, I still love Andrew.' She took a tissue from her soft leather bag and wiped her face. 'Pathetic, isn't it?'

'Not pathetic at all.' He stared ahead, in silence for a moment, his hands resting on the steering wheel. Should he tell her? Maybe not. It was none of his business. But what the hell? 'Andrew could certainly do with someone on his side at the moment. He's thinking of giving up, you know. Says there's no point carrying on the business now.'

Jane turned to him in astonishment. 'Give up the business? But it's Andrew's life. I can't believe it.'

'I can,' Nick said. 'When you lose someone you love, it kind of shakes you to the very foundations of your being, so you lose all sense of perspective. Of who you are. What you are. Where you are, even. It's like . . . ' He struggled to find the right metaphor to describe his life after Abbie and the baby had died. 'It's like those houses that are built on stilts. Everything's fine and normal until one day when something comes along and knocks out those stilts, and the whole house sinks down into the water. Suddenly, everything's changed. The way you think, the way you feel — everything. Nothing is ever the same.' He paused and shook his head. 'Sorry, didn't mean to bore you.'

'You didn't,' she said quietly. 'You've given me much food for thought. Thank you for being so honest with me. And I am so very sorry for your loss.'

'And I for yours.'

She sighed. 'Grief can be such an isolating emotion, can't it? Most of the time you just want to shut yourself away and not have to think about anyone or anything else. I'll go and see Andrew tomorrow. See if I can catch him on his own. Now, this has been a harrowing day for all of us, and I wasn't kidding about the jet lag. I think I'd like to go back to my hotel now.'

Nick, too, needed time alone. It had indeed been a harrowing day for everyone. But his last thought, as sleep finally caught up with him that night, was of Caitlin, and the haunted look in her eyes when he'd told her how the police had found *Storm Chaser*.

24

I woke up to the ringing of my phone. For a moment I lay there, my heart pounding, my body tensed. Would this be the one? The call from the police to say they'd found Liam's body?

Then I remembered. There would be no such call. Liam was alive. And the joy that flooded my body was so intense I could hardly speak.

'Caitlin? It's Nick. I'm just calling to see if you're all right.'

'Oh Nick, I'm more than all right.' I cleared my throat, emotion making it difficult to speak. 'It's Liam. He's home. He's OK.'

There was a stunned silence. Then: 'Liam's OK? But that's fantastic. When did this happen?'

'Yesterday afternoon. Just as Dad and I were psyching ourselves up to go to the police station, Liam walked in.'

Briefly, I told him Liam's story. A story that, no doubt, I was going to be repeating many times in the days ahead. A story I would never tire of telling.

'Amazing,' he said. 'You and Joe must be so relieved.'

'Relieved isn't the word for it. In fact, there's not a single word to cover how I feel. Relief, joy, intense happiness, an overwhelming desire to strangle him . . . all that and more.'

'I can imagine. I'm so pleased for you, Caitlin. I really am. And for your father.'

'Thanks,' I said. Then, before I could change my mind, I went on, 'Look, I don't know if you're doing anything this morning, but Liam's going down to Poole today to see if he can straighten things out with your friend. And Dad . . . well, he'll be in the boat house as usual, doing what he always does when things get a bit much for him — burying himself in work. But he's still very shaken, of course. So I thought I'd take the dog out for a couple of hours, and wondered if you'd like to come. Of course, I expect you're busy, and — '

'I'd love to,' he said. 'I could do with blowing a few cobwebs away.'

'In that case, I know just the place if you don't mind driving. It's one of Archie's favourite walks. And I can promise you it's one of the best views in Dorset if the weather holds up.'

But it didn't. The sky was dark and threatening as we headed along the coast road towards Abbotsbury. 'Where are you taking me?' he said as we turned off the main road and into a narrow lane where his car brushed the hedges on both sides.

'You'll see. You can park over there. Better hang on to your hat when you get out, though. It can be pretty windy up here.'

'Lucky I'm not planning on wearing one then,' he said as he parked. As he opened the boot to get his walking boots out, I noticed a red rope coiled neatly in the back. He saw me looking and grinned.

'I do a spot of rock climbing back home,' he said. 'Although I don't suppose there's much chance of that around here.'

'I'm afraid not. Certainly not in this area; the cliffs are too crumbly for climbing. But we can still offer some good, challenging walks. This one's pretty easy, though.'

Archie knew exactly where he was going and bounded off like a puppy, while Nick and I followed at a more sedate pace along a wide grassy path that stretched for miles along the ridge of a hill. I drew in deep lungfuls of air, and for the first time in what seemed like forever felt the last of the tension that had become a part of me for so long finally drain away.

'What is this place?' Nick asked.

'It's part of the South Dorset Ridgeway, and it's a pity you're not seeing it on a better day. The views down across the Fleet towards Portland are fantastic, but I'm afraid you'll have to take my word for it today.'

The wind was blowing straight in our faces, snatching our words and making conversation difficult. But it didn't matter. I felt a bubble of happiness well up in me that was so strong I was in danger of breaking into that Julie Andrews moment in *The Sound of Music* when she goes running around the mountain singing about the hills being alive.

'What's so funny?' Nick had to shout to make himself heard.

'I was debating whether to do my Julie Andrews impression but decided to spare you. Besides, Archie would only join in, and his singing's worse than mine.' I looked across at the storm clouds that were gathering out at sea. 'But I think we'd better head back. That lot out there is heading our way. And quickly.'

We turned back. It was a lot easier on the way back, as we had the wind behind us. It also made conversation easier, and Nick was an entertaining walking companion.

As the path crossed a sheep-studded field, I was pointing out one of the many round barrows that are to be found along this ancient path that has been used by travellers for hundreds of years, when I caught my foot in a rabbit hole and would have pitched forward had Nick not caught me.

For a long moment we stayed as if frozen, his arm around my waist, our faces just inches apart. I had every intention of making some flip comment, but the words died as soon as they formed.

What would happen, I wondered, if I moved closer to him? Would he shrink back, or did he feel the same pull of attraction that I felt? Was his heart hammering in his chest the same way mine was? His grey-blue eyes seemed to darken as he looked down at me.

But before either of us could move, down came the first heavy spots of rain. Talk about timing. We'd either been on the brink of something good, or I'd been about to make a complete fool of myself. Again.

For once, I was glad of the rain. We called Archie away from his in-depth investigations into rabbit holes and hurried back to the car as the rain started lashing down.

'How's Andrew?' I said quickly the moment we got in the car, hoping by doing so I'd made it obvious that I didn't want to talk about what had so nearly happened back there. 'I thought he bore up pretty well yesterday, considering.'

He paused for a second, then started the car. 'He's very good at putting on a brave face. But it's broken him. I'm really quite worried about him.'

'I'm sorry to hear that,' I said, touched by his obviously genuine concern for his employer.

'I shouldn't be telling you this,' he said, 'but you'll find out soon enough anyway. He's thinking of giving up.'

'What, the marina? His plans for Stargate?'

‘Everything. He says there’s no point carrying on with the business now he’s got no one to leave it to. He reckons he’s going to sell up and move somewhere warm.’

I swallowed nervously. Should I tell him about the baby? Not Nick, of course, but Andrew. Would he then think he had something, or rather someone, to carry on for?

‘I hope he doesn’t do anything hasty,’ I said.

‘It’s his decision,’ Nick said. ‘Would you like to stop somewhere for a coffee, or early lunch?’

‘Thanks, but I’d better get home and dry off.’ I wasn’t bothered about getting dried, of course. I needed to think about Andrew and whether or not I should tell him about the baby, sooner rather than the later I’d planned.

* * *

During the drive back from Stargate to drop Caitlin off, Nick cursed himself.

What was he thinking of, coming on to her like that? She was obviously still grieving for Ben. How could he have been so insensitive? No wonder she'd scuttled off like a scalded cat as soon as she got out of the car. She couldn't get away from him quick enough.

When Abbie died, he'd truly believed he would never again feel the pull of attraction towards another woman. And yet here he was, eighteen short months later, doing just that. How shallow did that make him? He and Abbie had met on their first day at secondary school and had been friends from that day on; then later, lovers. He'd always thought there would never be anyone who could replace her. And yet, here he was, less than two years later . . .

But there was something about Caitlin Mulryan, with her wild blue-black hair and freckled nose, and those sea-green eyes a man could lose himself in. There was something about the way they sparkled when she laughed that he simply could not get out of his head.

Time to go back to the office, get his head down and get on with some work, he reckoned. But before doing so, he needed to stop off in town to go to the bank. Too late, he remembered it was market day, and the normally wide pavements were crammed with stalls selling everything from fresh fish to phone covers to vintage clothes. As he dodged between the browsers, he almost collided with Jane Kington coming the other way.

'How are you today?' he asked.

'I'm just fine, thanks,' she said, although Nick judged from the dark circles under her eyes that even her carefully applied make-up failed to disguise that she was anything but. 'I'm sorry about yesterday. I don't usually weep all over virtual strangers who are just being kind.'

'It was a difficult day for all of us,' he said. 'Are you enjoying our local market? I have to say, it drives me nuts. I usually avoid town on market days. But I forgot that it's Wednesday today.'

'I know that feeling.' She smiled. 'No, street markets aren't my thing either. I was on my way to the travel agent's to see if I can bring my return flight forward.'

'When are you going back?'

They moved to one side as a woman with a double pram edged past them, scraping Nick's ankles as she did so.

'As soon as I can get a flight,' Jane said. 'There's no point staying any longer.'

Nick hesitated. Should he tell her or not? Probably should. But not here in all this mayhem.

'Have you time for a coffee?' he said. 'There's a very nice place just up the road. A decent cup of coffee and some peace and quiet guaranteed.'

'Sounds good to me,' she said.

The coffee and the peace and quiet were everything Nick had promised. Jane took a sip of the strong, rich coffee and leaned back into the squashy leather armchair with a relaxed sigh.

'There's been a development,' Nick

said, 'that I think you should be aware of.'

'What sort of development?' She put her cup down and looked at him warily.

'Have you heard that Liam Mulryan has turned up alive and well?'

'Liam?' She straightened up, her face pale beneath her tan. 'After all this time? I don't understand. What happened? Where has he been? Why didn't he come forward sooner?' She fired questions at him like bullets.

'Apparently he was concussed in the explosion and washed up further down the coast, where someone took him in. He only knew Ben had died when he saw the report of the inquest in an old paper.'

'That's . . . ' Her fingers worried at the fine gold chain at her throat. 'That's just . . . I can't take it in. Liam. Alive. I'm pleased for his family. Of course I am. But it's such a shock.'

'I'm sorry. I can see this has shaken you. Shall I take you back to your hotel?'

She shook her head. 'No. No. I've got to think. About Andrew.' She put her hand to her mouth and he had to strain to hear her. 'What do you think this will do to Andrew when he finds out?'

'To be honest, I don't know. I was thinking of going up there and telling him. If he doesn't know already, of course.'

'Do you think he might?'

Nick shrugged. 'This is a small place. News travels fast.'

'I'll tell him,' she said slowly. 'I'll go up there now and tell him.'

'But your travel plans?'

'Are not important,' she said, her voice suddenly brisk and determined, her shoulders straighter. 'What is important is that Andrew shouldn't be on his own at this time. Especially now, after all he's been through in the last couple of weeks. I want to make sure he's all right.'

'I'll give you a lift then.'

'That's very kind of you. You know, Nick, what you said last night about how everything changes when you lose someone you love — I've been thinking about that. I want to be there for Andrew, whether he wants me there or not. This time he's not going to send me away.'

25

News of Liam's return spread around Stargate and the surrounding district like forest fire. So, too, the news that Andrew Kington had given up on the marina project and was thinking of leaving the area.

Dad and Liam tiptoed around each other like polite strangers, but there was no more I'll-never-forgive-you rhetoric bouncing around the place, which was progress of a sort.

After a lot of thought, Liam told the police about the fight between him and Ben in the boat house. But they said it was nothing to do with them, and the hunted look in Liam's eyes began to fade like his bruises.

Then, soon after returning Lazarus-like to our lives, he left again, this time to start his new job in Poole, where a rush of orders had them desperate for him to start as soon as possible.

'But you're not getting rid of me that easily,' he said. 'I'll be back at weekends. So don't you go moving into my room the minute I've gone, Cait.'

The sun was glinting on the water and the soaring, shrieking gulls were brilliant white against the deep blue of the sky as Dad, Archie and I stood outside the house and watched Liam drive away. Archie pressed into my side with a little whimper, and I promised him his favourite walk later and assured him that Liam would be back at the weekend.

Dad's eyes had the same sad look as Archie's as he watched Liam's car disappear around the corner, but I didn't think a long walk and a Bonio would work for him.

'It's what he wants to do, Dad,' I said quietly.

'Sure. I couldn't be happier for the boy and that's a fact,' he said with a forced brightness that didn't fool me for a nanosecond. 'I'm just sorry that he didn't say sooner about not being happy here. We could have sorted something out. Instead of which — '

'Instead of which, he's alive and well and doing something he loves. Be happy for him, Dad.' I squeezed his arm and went for a change of subject instead of going down the same old road we'd been down so many times since Liam's return. 'So, are you going to rebuild *Storm Chaser*?'

He shook his head. 'I'm selling the boatyard to pay off my debts.'

'Are you saying Andrew is still pushing you for the loan repayment?'

He shook his head. 'On the contrary. I had a letter from his accountant this morning saying that, owing to what he called an administrative error, there appeared to have been an overpayment on my part, and enclosed was a fairly handsome cheque.'

'That's great news, but I don't get it. Why do you have to sell the boatyard?' Trying to imagine my dad without the boatyard was like thinking of Marks without Spencer or Batman without Robin. 'What would you do instead?'

He shrugged. 'Who knows? Take tourists mackerel fishing. Sell ice cream. Anything.'

'Do you *want* to sell? Is that it? Now that Liam isn't working with you?' I looked at him and frowned. 'Dad? This isn't a bit of emotional blackmail on your part to get Liam to come back, is it? Because if so — '

'No, of course it's not,' he said with a flash of his old spirit. 'I'm happy for the lad, honest I am.'

'Then is it because you can't manage the work without him? Liam always said he did the majority of the strong-arm stuff,' I added with a smile, knowing — or rather hoping — that it would set him off and chase away the emptiness in his eyes. It worked.

'Can't manage without him — ? I'll have you know, young lady, I'm good for another thirty-odd years, so I am, and I'll thank you not to be putting me out to pasture just yet.'

It was good to see a bit of the old spark back and we smiled easily at each other, the way we used to. But, too soon, the shadows came back to his face.

'Seriously though, sweetheart, I've no choice but to sell the boatyard. It's nothing to do with Liam or Andrew Kington's loan. I have to pay *Storm Chaser*'s owner back his advance. I'm surprised the fellow hasn't been pushing me. He's being remarkably patient about the whole thing.'

'Is that all?' I said before I could stop myself. I thought of Maggie's unstinting generosity, not just to Dad but the entire Mulryan family. The way she'd always been there for each and every one of us. She had, indeed, been remarkably patient.

'All? That's more than enough, wouldn't you say? Liam was right about one thing: I should never have taken the job on in the first place. Anonymous customer, indeed. No wonder my son thought I was losing it. He was probably right. But it was just . . . well, when I first saw what the fellow wanted for *Storm Chaser*, it was like I'd written those specs myself.' Dad's eyes shone like I hadn't seen them shine for a long, long time. 'It was the boat I'd always dreamt of building. I couldn't say no, whatever daft clauses the fellow chose to put on it.'

'Look, before you do anything drastic, why don't you talk to Maggie about it first?' I said, not wanting to betray Maggie's confidence but desperate to get the two of them talking to each other. 'I always find she's the perfect person to talk through a problem with. You know how sensible and practical she is. Who knows — she may even come up with a solution, a way for you to rebuild *Storm Chaser*. Promise me you'll talk to her, Dad. Please?'

'Now why would I be doing that? She must be getting pretty fed up with the whole damn lot of us Mulryans by now. In fact, I wouldn't be surprised to see the For Sale signs go up on her house any day now.'

'Don't be silly. She loves Stargate. She'd never leave the place. Or you,' I added quietly, not sure if he'd heard me or not.

He turned to go back into the house, but not before I'd caught the look on his face. If I hadn't known better, I'd have thought my gruff, I-can't-be-doing-with-all-that-nonsense father was blushing.

'She wouldn't mind, you know,' I said gently as I caught up with him and gave him a big hug.

'Mind what? Maggie doesn't — '

'I meant Mum. She wouldn't mind about you and Maggie. And Liam and I certainly don't.'

He stepped away from me, his face redder than ever, his eyes moist. 'Maggie's a good neighbour, that's all. There is no me and Maggie, as you put it. Now I can't stand around here all day talking, even if you can. I've got things to do.'

'Dad, wait. Listen to me for once, will you? You say there's no Maggie and you. But you'd like there to be, wouldn't you?' I persisted, convinced the two of them would go on pussyfooting around each other until the cows came home unless someone gave them a nudge.

'Well, she's — '

'A warm, intelligent woman who never stopped loving you. Not even when you married her best friend.'

He looked startled. 'Now how would you be knowing that?'

'Some of the things she's said — and didn't say.' I took a chance and went for the Big One. 'Goodness knows why, but she still loves you.'

'Ah now, you're wrong there.' He couldn't look me in the eye. Instead, he tilted his head and watched the gulls as they wheeled across the sky, shrieking at each other like noisy teenagers hitting the town on a Saturday night. 'I'll not deny she had feelings for me back when we were both young and foolish. But I broke her heart — and her father's — and she's never forgiven me.'

I put my hand on his arm. 'That's where you're wrong. Maggie doesn't go in for these long-held grudges.'

He turned to look at me, his eyes full of pain. 'Unlike me, you mean. I've been a right fool, haven't I?'

'No, you haven't. Andrew Kington said and did some terrible things to you. And you'd every right to be angry with him. But don't you think it's time to let it go? This baby of mine isn't just your grandchild, it's his too. And I'll not have the two of you scrapping over him like you've scrapped over everything else.'

'So you're going to tell Kington about the baby, are you?' There was a spark of the old anger in his eyes.

'Of course I am. I don't know how he's going to feel about it. But I thought maybe the knowledge that something of Ben lives on might bring him some comfort one day. I'm going to see him, Dad. And you're not going to stop me.'

He gave me a long, steady look, then opened his arms and pulled me to his chest. 'I wouldn't dream of it, darling girl,' he said.

'Good,' I said. Then, making the most of the moment, I went on, 'I'm going to take Archie for a walk now. You go and see Maggie. Do it now. Tell her how about how you're thinking of selling the boatyard and how you feel about her. Tell her — '

'Now that's enough, young lady,' he said firmly.

And I rather hoped it was.

* * *

Maggie looked up from her laptop and waved at Caitlin as she went past with Archie. Joe was outside too, and even from this distance Maggie could see he was deep in thought as he watched Caitlin disappear around the corner. But then instead of going to the boat house as she'd expected, he turned and came towards her house. He looked up, saw her watching him from her study window, and motioned that he wanted to speak to her.

'Joe? Is anything wrong?' she asked as she opened the door.

'Now why should there be anything wrong?' he said. 'Can't a man visit his neighbour?'

'No. I mean yes, of course he can. Come on into the kitchen and I'll put the kettle on.'

He followed her in and stood on the other side of her large kitchen table, jingling the loose change in his pocket, a small frown creasing his forehead. She reached for the kettle and filled it with water, unsettled by tension that radiated from him.

'Have you decided what you're going to do about *Storm Chaser*?' she asked. 'Are you going to rebuild her?'

He sighed. 'I'm not sure I can afford to, Maggie. And that's a fact. But I didn't come here to talk about that. At least, not directly.'

'You didn't?' Her unease deepened by the intense way he was looking at her, and she took her time getting a couple of cheerful yellow mugs down from the hooks on her old Welsh dresser.

'It was something Caitlin said. About how I should talk over my problems with you. About *Storm Chaser*'s mysterious, anonymous customer who is, it appears, in no hurry to have his — or maybe her — advance returned, even though the boat is in hundreds of pieces, thanks to my reckless son.'

'Still, Liam's safe. That's all that matters.'

'And there's not a minute in the day when I don't thank God for it.' His voice shook with barely controlled emotion.

'*Storm Chaser*'s a good boat, Joe. Your clever design saved Liam's life. I really think you should rebuild her.'

'And what will you do with it when I have done so, Maggie?' he said softly.

'Extend the tearoom by offering to take tourists out for a trip around the bay, with a cream tea thrown in for good measure?'

'Me?' Heat surged into her face. 'Why would I?'

'It was you, wasn't it? You put up the money for *Storm Chaser*. Why didn't you tell me?'

Maggie turned away, thankful for the shrill of the kettle to give her time to think of her answer. She reached for the teapot, but Joe moved it beyond her grasp.

'Forget the tea. I'm not here for that. Just answer my question.'

'I didn't tell you because I thought if you knew it was me, you'd refuse the money,' Maggie said, her face still burning. 'I know what a stiff-necked, proud so-and-so you can be. Besides, this was one way I could repay the debt I owed you for what my father did to you all those years ago.'

It was such a relief to be able to say the words she'd kept bottled up inside her for so many years; to release some of the guilt she'd carried around with her all that time. 'If he hadn't insisted you pay him the money for the business in full when we . . . when we split up,' she went on, 'you'd never have got yourself in debt with Andrew Kington with such terrible results. I'm sorry, Joe. I'm really, really sorry.'

He stared at Maggie, his eyes wide with shock. For once in his life, Joe Mulryan appeared to be completely lost for words. Maggie's heart sank. What had she been thinking of, raking all that old story up? Wasn't she the one always telling him to let go of the past? What sort of an idiot did that make her?

'Joe?' Her voice was little more than a whisper. 'I'm sorry if I've upset you. But I've felt so guilty about this, for so long.'

'Guilty? So is that why you've been so good to us all these years? Always ready to help out with the kids, particularly when my sister had enough of them and hightailed it back to

Ireland; the money for the boat. Was all that because you felt guilty?'

Maggie took a deep breath, conscious of the fact that what she said next could well affect the rest of her life. Ever since Joe had broken things off with her to marry Helen, she'd been afraid of showing her feelings, preferring instead to pour all her emotion into her writing.

But this wasn't fiction; this was real life, and there was no guaranteed happy-ever-after ending. It was time for her to take the biggest gamble of her life.

'I didn't do it out of guilt, Joe,' she said steadily. 'I did it because I love Liam and Caitlin. They couldn't be dearer to me if they were my own children. And . . . ' She took a steadying breath, but her voice still shook as she went on. ' . . . I love you. From that very first day you sailed into Stargate. I love you, Joe Mulryan. I always have. I always will. There, I've said it. Well, go on then, say something.'

But there are times when words are

not needed. With a shaky sigh, Joe pulled Maggie into his arms, smoothed back her hair and gave her a long, loving kiss. It was as if time had rolled back and Maggie felt she'd come home at last.

The kettle hissed on the hob, and the only other sound in the kitchen was the tinkle of hairpins as they fell to the floor.

26

Nick's car was in the car park of The Sailor's Return as I went past with Archie. My heart gave a little skip and, on an impulse, I went in. Since the day along the Ridgeway, we'd shared several walks together, although I'd been been careful to keep things on a purely friendly footing after that brief moment of madness. Did I wish it had gone any further? I had no idea; I only knew that I got little fluttery feelings in my stomach that had nothing to do with the morning sickness I was beginning to experience. There was also a voice in my head nagging at me to tell him I was pregnant before we got in any deeper.

He was in the bar talking to the landlord, a set of plans spread across the table in front of them. Both men looked up as I came in.

'Hi, Nick. I was going to ask you if

you were up to a cliff walk over Golden Cap, but I can see you're busy.'

Nick was a keen walker and was always going on about the delights of his native Yorkshire, so I felt duty-bound to show him that anything Yorkshire could do, Dorset could do better.

Nick folded up the plans. 'We're done here, aren't we, Mike? And I am allowed a lunch hour, you know. I've got my walking boots in the car. Will I need them?'

'Probably. The path can be slippery in places, particularly after all the rain we've had recently. But I'll warn you, it's quite a climb. It's the highest point on the south coast, you know.'

He laughed. 'You soft southerners don't know what a climb is. Wait until I show you Whernside. Hang on then while I get my boots.'

My heart did a funny little skip at his casual reference to the future. Did he mean *our* future? I bit my lip in an agony of indecision while the nagging voice inside my head rose to a crescendo. I could put it off no longer. I followed him across to his car and as he picked up his boots, I took a deep breath.

'Nick.' I twisted Archie's lead around my fingers. 'There's something I have to tell you.'

His eyes were wary as he turned towards me, alerted by the tone of my voice. 'That sounds pretty serious.'

'Yes, it is,' I said. 'But in a good way. At least for me,' I added, and was surprised to find I really meant it.

'You won the lottery?' His attempt to lighten the tension that had suddenly sprung up between us didn't quite work.

I pressed my hands together so hard, Archie's lead dug into my palm. 'I'm pregnant.'

He stepped back as if I'd struck him. His mouth tightened. No sign of a smile now. No flicker of kindness. He stared at me, his eyes as dark as a stormy night sky. They were the eyes of an angry stranger, not the man I was falling in love with.

'I . . . I just thought you should know,' I stammered.

'What made you think I'd be interested?' His voice was glacial.

'Well, we . . . I . . . '

'I suppose it's Ben's?'

'Yes. Of course.'

'And you had me all lined up as the next patsy, did you?'

'Patsy?' For one wild second, I couldn't work out what he was saying. 'Sorry? I don't know what you mean.'

'Oh, I rather think you do. That's what all this has been all about, isn't it? Well, sorry, lady — you can come on to me all you like, but I'm not buying.' He threw his boots into the back of the car and slammed the lid shut with such ferocity the car shook. Archie whimpered and pushed himself into my legs, his body trembling, his tail beating an anxious tattoo.

I froze, too shocked to speak or to reassure the dog. I didn't even move when Nick took off with such force the wheels sprayed pinpricks of gravel over us and Archie tugged on the lead to get away from it.

My brain caught up a moment too late. He'd thought I was telling him because I was on the hunt for a father for my baby. He thought I'd 'come on to' him, as he'd so charmingly phrased it, in a deliberate attempt to trap him.

How dare he! Of all the sanctimonious, unbearable idiots. Why had I ever thought I was in love with him? How could I have been so spectacularly wrong about him? And what was the matter with me that I chose one wrong one after another? First Matt, then Ben. And now Nick.

But I'd really thought Nick was different. In fact, I'd come dangerously close to falling in love with him. What a good job he'd shown his true colours before I'd taken that last step.

I hadn't expected him to be over the moon about my pregnancy. I certainly hadn't been looking for a father for my baby. I was just trying to be honest with him.

And yet, that small voice inside my head — the one I really, really wished would just shut up and go away — prompted, *What did you expect him to do? Clasp you in his arms and say that it doesn't matter that you're carrying another man's child? After all, you let him believe you were in love with Ben so that he wouldn't think too badly of you. Now you want him to believe that you've fallen out of love with Ben and in love with him in the few short weeks since Ben's death? No wonder he stormed off.*

How could I have been so stupid? Not for telling him; that had to be done, whatever the consequences. My stupidity lay in falling in love — properly in love, for the first and last time in my life — with the man who'd just looked at me like I'd crawled out from under a stone. Because it was no good trying to fool myself anymore: I was in love with Nick. How was that for the ultimate in stupidity?

If only. I was back to those two sad words again. If only it had been Nick in the bar of the Sailor's that night and not Ben. How different things would have been — for everyone.

'Sorry, Archie,' I said as we walked back home. 'No walk up Golden Cap today, boy, I'm afraid. And if my day's started this badly, I might as well go and tell Andrew Kington my news.'

I borrowed Dad's rattly old van and drove up to Andrew's clifftop house. At any other time it would have made me laugh to see Dad's scruffy old wreck parked alongside Andrew's sleek, top-of-the-range BMW. Instead, I froze and almost turned back as I recognised Nick's car also parked on the long sweep of gravel in front of the triple garage. Had he raced up here to tell Andrew about the baby? Surely not.

I forced myself to keep walking up to the front door. My bad feeling got a whole lot worse when it opened and Nick stood there, his eyes as cold and distant as before.

'I'm afraid you've had a wasted journey,' he said, moving to close the door. 'Andrew's not seeing anyone at the moment. Certainly not you.'

'He's got a right to know, Nick. And I'll thank you to keep out of this. It's nothing to do with you.'

'A right to know what?'

Nick and I both jumped as Andrew Kington came up unexpectedly behind us. I'd assumed he was somewhere in the house, but instead he'd come from the garden.

I was shocked at the change in him. He'd looked bad enough at the funeral, but now it was like he was wasting away. And his pale grey eyes had that cold, glazed look more often seen on a fishmonger's slab.

'Can I come in?' I asked.

He nodded. Nick went to walk away but he called him back. 'I'd like you to stay, please. I prefer a witness when dealing with a Mulryan.'

'Mr Kington, please.' I ignored the

jibe and focused instead on keeping my voice measured and steady, despite what felt like a hundred butterflies flitting madly around inside me. 'What I have to say is very personal and private.'

'All the more reason for Nick to stay. Come along in, the pair of you.'

Nick and I exchanged glares as we followed him down a long wood-panelled passageway into a room with large glazed doors that opened onto a rose garden. It was obviously his study, dominated as it was by the largest and tidiest desk I'd ever seen. He motioned us to a couple of chairs ranged opposite the desk and seated himself in an intimidating black leather chair that looked as if it had come off the *Mastermind* set.

'Well then, Caitlin? What is it that I have a right to know?'

I took a deep breath and tried to remember what I'd rehearsed at least fifty times during the short drive up here. I'd made a complete mess of telling Nick. I didn't want to make the same mistake with this brittle-looking man who looked as if he'd shatter into a thousand pieces if I did.

'First, I'd like to say how sorry I am about Ben.'

A spot of colour stained his pale cheeks. 'I heard Liam was back. The luck of the Irish, eh?' He caught himself. 'Forgive me; I shouldn't have said that. I understand Joe's well-designed boat saved him. I'm happy for you.' But he looked like he'd never be happy again.

I swallowed hard and prayed for the right words. 'Mr Kington, before I go any further, I want you to know I don't want anything from you. Not a penny.'

They were not the right words, obviously. It was like a shutter had come down across his hooded eyes, and the look he and Nick exchanged seemed to say, *See? We were right. This is a shakedown*.

'Go on,' he said coldly.

'I thought you ought to know. I'm

having a baby. Ben's baby.'

I felt Nick stiffen beside me, heard Andrew's sharp intake of breath, and smelt the sugared-almond fragrance of roses drifting in through the open doors. Nobody moved. Nobody spoke. Andrew didn't take his eyes off my face. Nick, on the other hand, looked anywhere except at me.

I cleared my throat and forced myself on. 'I'm only telling you because you've a right to know. I realise this has come as a shock. But I thought one day you might find some comfort from the knowledge that Ben lives on in my child.'

'Did you love my son?'

'We were . . . very close.' I chose my words with care and forced myself to remember Ben as he'd been the night in the bar: warm, funny, and affectionate. Not the snarling, vindictive stranger of the morning after who'd so nearly cost my brother his life.

Andrew was very still. Very silent.

I stood up. 'As I said, I don't want

anything from you, and am willing to sign any paper your lawyers wish to draw up to that effect. Also, if you want to do a DNA test on the baby after he's born, I'll understand.'

'You're carrying a boy?' For a brief second something flickered in those cold, dead eyes.

'It's too early to say. Would you like me to keep you informed?'

He shook his head. 'I don't know. I can't take it in.'

I stood up and put a piece of paper on his desk. 'My mobile. I shan't be leaving Stargate. At least, not before the baby's born.'

I stumbled slightly as I walked away. My knees had turned to water and I prayed they'd hold out long enough for me to reach Dad's van without making a complete fool of myself. Nick was across the room and at my side in an instant. But I waved him away.

'I'll see myself out,' I said sharply. 'I think you should stay with Mr Kington.'

As I walked across the wide entrance hall, someone was coming down the wide oak stairs. The last person I expected to see.

'Are you all right?' Jane Kington peered at me anxiously. 'You look quite unwell.'

I nodded. 'I'm fine,' I said. 'But I'm afraid I've just given your . . . your husband a shock. I think you should go to him. He's in the study.'

She hurried away and I let myself out of the too-large, too-quiet house. Though the heavy silence was shattered all too soon by the screeching protest of Dad's old van firing reluctantly into life.

27

Andrew was slumped at his desk, his head in his hands, but straightened up quickly as Jane came into the room.

'Andrew? I've just seen Joe Mulryan's girl leave the house looking like she'd just seen a ghost. What have you been saying to the poor child?'

Nick could barely contain himself. Poor child, indeed!

'What are you still doing here?' Andrew snapped without answering her question. 'I thought I told you last night to go.'

'And I thought I told you last night that I'm going nowhere until I'm satisfied that you're looking after yourself properly. Have you eaten this morning?'

'What I eat is no concern of yours,' he said. 'You gave up that right a long time ago.'

Nick got up to go. The last thing he wanted was to be caught up in the middle of a full-on domestic between his employer and his ex. He was glad he'd come, though. He'd had a feeling Caitlin was on her way up here and he'd wanted to be around just in case, so had called in on the pretext of bringing some papers that needed Andrew's signature. He was relieved to see that Jane had been as good as her word and was sticking around, whether Andrew wanted her to or not. He was worried about Andrew, and Caitlin Mulryan's bombshell had done nothing to lessen that worry. Quite the contrary.

This was no place for him right now, though. He felt a pang of regret for the walk Caitlin had promised him. He could do with a blast of fresh air after the stifling, overheated atmosphere of Andrew's house.

A walk up Golden Cap. Another lifetime. Another Caitlin.

'Well, if you'll excuse me, I'll be off,' he said, and moved towards the door.

As he did so, he was surprised to see Jane come with him.

'Caitlin Mulryan told me she'd just given Andrew a shock,' she said as they reached the front door. 'He won't even tell me whether or not he's had breakfast, so he's hardly likely to tell me what it is. Will you? I need to know if there's anything I can do to help him, Nick.'

Nick was about to say that it wasn't his place to tell her. But then he thought better of it. After all, she had as big a stake in all this as Andrew did.

'She came to tell him she's pregnant,' Nick said curtly. 'And that the baby is Ben's.'

For a moment, Jane too was speechless. She looked intently at Nick, her eyes boring into his. 'Ben's baby? She's having Ben's baby? Is she sure?'

'She seemed pretty sure to me.'

'And how has Andrew taken it?'

'You've just seen. Shocked, just like you. He can't really take it in. She assured him she wants nothing from him. But . . . ' He shrugged and spread his hands.

Suddenly a smile spread across her face, chasing the lines of strain from her face. 'A baby. Ben's baby. But that's wonderful.'

'Wonderful?' Nick scowled. What was it about women and babies that made simple common sense fly out of the window the moment they were mentioned? 'You think it's wonderful?'

'Yes, of course. Don't you?' She looked at him intently. 'Don't you see what a difference this could make to Andrew? How it gives him something to live for?'

'That's what Caitlin said,' Nick said, remembering not only her words but the pallor of her skin and the way her hand had slid to her stomach in an instinctive, protective gesture that he knew so well, as she'd said them.

'But you're not happy about it, are you?' Jane said quietly. 'Were you and Caitlin involved? Or maybe still are involved? Is that what's eating you up inside?'

'I don't know what you mean.' Nick put his hand on the door but Jane stopped him.

'I rather think you do,' she said. 'I've seen the way you look at her. The way she looks at you. Listen, Nick, you gave me food for thought the other night. Now I'd like to reciprocate. I don't know what went on between Ben and Caitlin, but don't let it spoil things for you two.'

'There is no us two, as you put it,' he said. 'Now, if you'll excuse me, I've got a hundred and one things to do back at the office.'

Things like clearing up a few outstanding items, looking up the terms of his contract with Andrew to see what it would cost him to break it, then getting as far away from Stargate — not to mention Caitlin Mulryan and her baby — as he could.

* * *

I can't remember much about the drive back home from Andrew's house, only that I was still shaking and on the verge of tears when I let myself in. I went straight into the kitchen, sat down at the table, and put my head in my hands while I tried to regain some control. Had I done the right thing telling Andrew about the baby? Had I made things worse for him?

He'd just sat there like a statue. But what had I expected — that he was going to throw his arms around me and cry for joy? Of course I hadn't. I'd known it was going to be difficult. But to have to do it with Nick there, sitting so close to me that I could feel the heat of his barely suppressed anger and disapproval, made it one of the most difficult things I'd ever done. How I'd stopped myself from running out of that room, I'll never know.

Archie padded across and laid his head in my lap with one of those deep isn't-life-awful sighs he specialises in. I smoothed back the rough hair above his eyes where his eyebrows sprouted in all directions, trying, but failing as always, to get it to lie in some sort of order.

Not that I was any more successful at getting the thoughts in my head in any better order. The only thing I was thankful for was that Dad was out, probably in the boat house. If he came in, he'd see right away somethi[illegible]tter wrong, and I wasn't ready to tel[illegible] to an Not until I had sorted it out in m[illegible]eep mind first.

The first spots of rain hitting the window made my mind up. A walk along the cliff path in the rain. Perfect. That would suit my mood, and I still owed Archie a walk. There is something exhilarating about watching the storm-tossed waves crashing onto the shore and hearing the roar and hiss over the pebbles. Especially now I knew my brother wasn't lying somewhere down there.

'Come on then,' I called Archie, shrugging on my waterproof and setting off in the rain, not even bothering to put my hood up. I had already decided on the path I was going to take. Call it rubbing salt in a wound, but that was the mood I was in.

I took the footpath that led along the cliffs towards Golden Cap, the route I'd planned to take with Nick that morning. The sun had been shining [illegible] Nick had been smiling, and I had [illegible] happy. But it wasn't true happi[illegible] was it? Because I knew I had to tell him. And I didn't regret telling him; only the fact that I hadn't done it sooner. Before I'd fallen in love with him.

I had such a lot to be happy about, after all, I told myself sternly as I strode along. Liam was safe and well and starting his dream job. My baby would, I hoped, in time make a difference to Andrew Kington's life and give him something to live for. And with a bit of luck, Dad and Maggie could well be sorting things out between them at long last. I should focus on all those good things and try to forget the contempt in

Nick's eyes. Who'd have thought he would turn out to be so judgemental? And so very, very wrong about me. How could he think that I was just trying to trap him?

As I carried on walking, the rain started coming down harder. The path was getting steeper and more slippery as Archie and I left the relative sh[illegible] of a wooded area and came out on[illegible] open stretch of cliff, where the sh[illegible] huddled together for shelter under a scrappy blackthorn hedge blown into strange, tortured shapes by the prevailing salt-laden wind.

But neither of us paid much heed to the weather. I was focused on my thoughts, Archie on flushing out the few hardy rabbits that had ventured out in the rain. Suddenly, he took off after one with a turn of speed that he hadn't put on in years.

'Archie! Come back!' I called after him, but the wind snatched my voice away. Still yelling at him, I hurried as fast as I could to get closer to him and put his lead back on, but he was having too much fun to pay any heed. His tail was up, ears flapping in the wind, long gangly legs skidding in all directions as he gave himself up completely to the thrill of the chase.

Suddenly, he was gone. He'd raced and chased along these cliff paths ever since he was a puppy. He knew every inch, every rabbit hole, and yet he'd disappeared over the edge.

'Archie! Archie!' I screamed, even though he couldn't hear me. At this point the path was a good twenty feet from the cliff edge, but it felt like twenty miles. As I ran towards the edge, my feet slipped on the slick, sheep-cropped grass and I landed heavily on my knees. I got up and forced myself to calm down. *Think clearly. There's no way I can help him if I have a broken ankle*.

After one of the wettest and stormiest winters in living memory, there'd been a number of cliff falls in the area over the course of the summer, with warnings of more to come. One of the falls, I knew, was somewhere on this stretch of cliff, although I hadn't been along here since it happened.

Archie had gone over on a part of the cliff with a fairly gradual descent down to a small, rocky beach that could only be safely reached from the sea. Liam and I had even climbed it once, although Dad would have skinned us alive and grounded us for the rest of our lives if he'd known. As I got closer, I prayed that there had been no falls here, and that there wasn't now a sheer drop to the rocks below.

I reached the edge, got down on my stomach and peered over.

'Oh God, oh no. Please, no.' There had, indeed, been a fall. Part of the sloping cliff face that Liam and I had so foolishly scrambled up had been sliced away, as if a giant knife had cut down through it like a piece of cake, cutting away the golden greensand stone which gives the cliff its famous colour, and revealing its slate-grey underbelly.

And Archie was cowering just feet away from it, looking shocked and frightened but, as far as I could tell, unharmed.

What to do? Oh God, what to do? He looked up at me and started to move towards me. As he did so, his movement dislodged still more rocks, which went bumping and banging their way down. Instinctively, he cowered down again. If I went down to help him, my additional weight would surely send both him and me crashing down.

'Stay there, Archie. Stay,' I shouted, praying that for once in his life the stupid dog would do as he was told.

I grabbed my phone and dialled Dad's number but, as always, his phone wasn't on and it went straight into voicemail. Who else to call? Liam was too far away. Maggie couldn't help. Mike in the pub had locked up and gone out for the afternoon.

There was only one thing for it.

'Nick,' I cried the moment he answered. 'Please, help me. It's Archie.

He's fallen over the cliff and I can't reach him.'

'Where are you?'

'I'm about a mile up the path that goes up by the side of the Sailor's towards Golden Cap. Just past the wooded section, where the cliff opens out. Please hurry. I'm trying to keep him calm and make him stay, but it's very slippery, and — '

'I'll be there in five. Stay calm.'

I don't know if he was there in five. I do know I didn't feel very calm, although I tried to appear so for Archie's sake. If anything happened to Archie, I'd never forgive myself. How could I have been so stupid, so self-centred that I hadn't thought to clip his lead on when we came out of the wood? I knew what he was like when he got scent of a rabbit.

'I'm so sorry, Archie,' I whispered. He was now huddled into the side of the cliff, his fur wet and spiky; but thankfully he was no longer trying to move.

After what seemed like forever — for once in my life I was too scared to keep track of time — I heard footsteps coming up the path. I looked back and almost cried with relief at the sight of Nick and my dad coming towards me. Nick was carrying the climbing rope I'd last seen in the back of his car.

'Damn fool dog,' Dad growled as he and Nick tied the rope to a nearby fence post. 'How did he get down there?'

'He was chasing a rabbit and just went over.' I gulped, panicky tears not far from the surface. 'This is all my fault. I should never — '

'No, you should never,' he said angrily. 'You stupid girl. When I saw Nick come hurtling down the road and he said you and Archie were up on the cliffs — in this weather — I couldn't believe it. How many years have you been walking these paths? What on earth made you come out in these conditions? Are you mad?'

'Right, Joe,' Nick's calm, authoritative voice cut across Dad's tirade. 'If you can steady the rope, I'll let myself down. Just feed it out and keep it as taut as you can; and if there's a slip, don't worry. It's tied to the post and I'll not fall very far. The main thing is the dog's quiet at the moment, and he's the right side of the landslip.'

'Be careful, won't you?' I said anxiously. 'It looks as if the bit Archie's on is set to go any minute.'

'I can see it. It's fine,' he said, then gave me a grin that even in my current frantic state made my heart flip. 'Don't worry. Call this a cliff? This is nothing to the ones we have up in Yorkshire, you know. It's a walk in the park.'

He made it look so easy. Slowly, cautiously, he made his way down, moving like a cat over the slippery surface, each step careful yet confident. He reached Archie without dislodging any more rocks. He had a bit of a job persuading the terrified dog to leave the ledge at first. But finally they began the agonisingly slow scramble back up the cliff with Dad and me hanging on to the rope.

My arms ached and the rope burned my hands where I was holding it so tightly, but the ground held as Nick and Archie inched their way back up, until finally Dad and I were able to reach down and grab the dog while Nick made it up the last few feet.

Finally, thankfully, they were both safely back on the path. We were all soaked to the skin, and Archie and Nick were both covered in mud as well.

'I don't know how to begin thanking you, Nick,' I said. 'If you hadn't answered the phone . . . '

'Well, I did. So let's not go there, shall we? The dog's safe, you're safe, that's all that matters. Come on, let's get you down and into some dry clothes.'

Dad, however, was less forgiving. 'Of all the stupid things you've done, Caitlin Mulryan — and goodness knows, girl, you and that harum-scarum brother of yours have done some stupid things in your time . . . ' he said, his voice raw with emotion. 'But this! This escapade was up there with the stupidest. That could have been you going over that cliff edge, girl, not the dog.'

'Never mind, Joe,' Nick said soothingly. 'There was no real harm done.'

But there was. Suddenly, the world spun around me. The ground came up to meet me as a searing pain like I'd never in my life experienced before twisted my stomach and bent me double.

My last thought before I lost consciousness was: how was I going to be able to tell Andrew Kington that I was losing Ben's baby?

28

The first thing I saw when I opened my eyes was a huge bunch of apricot roses on the locker by my bed. The second thing I noticed was Nick. He was sitting on the edge of a grey plastic chair, his head bent over a file of papers, a small frown of concentration creasing his forehead.

'Nick?' I began to move into a sitting position but he dropped the papers, put his hand on my shoulder and gently pushed me back into the bed. 'Don't try to move,' he said. 'Else you'll unhook all those things you're hooked up to.'

What things? I looked around, teetering on the edge of panic. Nothing made any sense. This wasn't my bedroom at home, and what was Nick doing here? And what was this tube thing in my arm? Then there was the harsh lighting, the unfamiliar bedcovers, the small white-walled room. And the smell — a weird combination of roses, toast, and antiseptic.

Then I remembered. The ambulance. The flashing lights. The hospital.

'Where's Dad?'

'I sent him down to the café for breakfast. He's been here all night with you. Do you want me to fetch him?'

'No.' It was a lie though, because I did want him. Very badly. I wanted to ask about the baby, but I didn't want to ask Nick. I remembered how he'd looked at me when I told him I was pregnant. I didn't want him to be the one to tell me I'd lost it.

'You're going to be OK,' he said, drawing his chair closer to the bed and leaning towards me.

I nodded. I had no words. There was no room in my head for anything but the one question I was too scared to ask.

He took my hand. 'Caitlin,' he said softly, 'you're both going to be OK. You and the baby. According to the doctor who spoke to your dad, you just need a few more days of complete bed rest and you'll both be fine.'

I sank back against the pillows, closed my eyes and gave myself up to the storm surge of relief that washed over me. Until that moment, I had no idea how desperately I wanted this unplanned, inconvenient, but so very precious baby. Not just for Andrew's sake, but my own as well.

'Thank you. Thank you.' My voice was barely above a whisper. The only thought in my head at that moment was that the baby was going to be all right. He was going to be all right. I promised I'd take better care of him, and myself, from now on.

I heard Nick stir in the seat beside me and finally opened my eyes. 'Are you OK?' he asked, his eyes full of concern. 'Do you want me to call a nurse?'

I shook my head. 'No, I'm fine, honestly. Just . . . ' I cleared my throat.

'Just trying to get my head together.' I looked across at the bunch of apricot roses on my locker. 'Are those from you?'

He shook his head. 'Jane Kington asked me to give them to you.'

'You told them? They must have been so worried.'

'Andrew doesn't know. But yes, Jane was worried. She'll be so relieved to know you're safe and well.'

'She knows about the baby?'

'She's thrilled,' Nick said, and my heart warmed towards her. And, of course, to the man sitting next to me. I didn't have a clue how I could begin thanking him for everything he'd done. But I had to try.

'Thank you, Nick. Thank you — for rescuing the dog and everything. I don't know what I'd have done if you hadn't been there.'

He stood up abruptly. 'Caitlin, don't,' he said quietly. 'You've nothing to thank me for, I promise you. I came to see you this morning because I need to tell you something, and your dad said he'd give me half an hour, which is just about up. So I'll quickly say what I've come here to say, then I'll leave you to get some rest.'

I wanted to ask him to stay but didn't. I braced myself for the news that he was leaving Stargate.

'What is it?' I asked.

'First off, I want to apologise. I behaved like a complete moron and said some terrible things to you. About the baby. Things that I should never have said and certainly didn't believe.' He sat down again, rested his elbows on his knees and stared at the floor. 'The thing is, after Abbie died, I really believed I would never be attracted to another woman again. But then you came along, with your wild hair, your green eyes and your bulging carrier bags and . . . and it was like you'd woken something inside me.'

'Nick, I — '

'No, please. Let me finish. I've been sitting here this last half an hour, working out how I was going to say this, and if you interrupt me I'll lose my thread. Did you know you snore, by the way?' he added with a sudden unexpected grin that took my breath away and released some of the tension that crackled in the air around us.

'I do not!'

'OK, sorry. Let me go on. There was something about you that I couldn't get out of my head, and I realised to my surprise that I was attracted to you. Which, after the first shock of surprise, wouldn't have been a problem. Abbie always said that if she died she wanted me to be happy again.'

'You talked about her dying?'

'She had a heart condition. It was discovered three months before we got married. We always knew The Big One, as she referred to it, could happen at any time, and Abbie was a very practical woman. Very . . . ' He paused. 'Very organised. Very used to getting her own way. That was why . . . ' He scratched his head. 'No, I'll come to that in a minute. Damn it, now I've lost my train of thought again. Where was I?'

'You, um . . . you said . . . ' Now it was my turn to hesitate.

He pushed his hands through his hair. 'OK, if you must know, I fancied you like hell. There, I've said it. But then, of course, I found out you were in love with Ben.'

'But I wasn't.' I knew he'd said not to interrupt, but I was desperate to make him understand. 'At least, I thought I was. But now I know I wasn't.' I took a deep breath. If I didn't say it now, I might never get the chance. And he had said he fancied me. Like hell. At least, he had at one time. But whatever he thought of me now, I really needed him to know.

'I was never really in love with Ben.' I couldn't look at him but focused instead on pleating the smooth white sheet in front of me. 'It was nothing more than a long-held schoolgirl crush coupled with too much alcohol and too little common sense. And, according to my mate at uni who did psychology, more than a little 'forbidden fruit'. Oh yes, I'd imagined myself in love with him for as long as I can remember. But it wasn't love. And the reason I know that is because it's nothing like what I feel for you. I love you, Nick. I'm sorry; you probably don't want to hear it. But it's the truth. If only we'd met at another time . . . If only you'd been in the bar of the Sailor's that night, and not Ben. Who knows?'

'Caitlin, I — '

'No — this time it's my turn to speak without interruption. I'm not asking for anything in return from you, Nick — least of all a father for my child. Dad and Maggie are being really cool about it and we'll manage just fine. Maggie has promised she'll help out with the childcare, so I can even go back to college next year to do my teacher training. I let you believe I was in love with Ben because . . . ' I swallowed. This was harder than I thought.

'Because I didn't want you to think that I was the sort of tarty girl who went in for one-night stands. Which, of course, was exactly what it was.'

Nick stared at me, the expression in his eyes unreadable.

'I just wanted you to know, that's all,' I said, my cheeks scarlet, my fingers still working away at the sheet. 'Thank you for saving Archie yesterday, and for all you've done for me. But I think you'd better go now.'

'I think I'd better not,' he said. 'The first thing you need to know is that I never believed you were looking for a father for the baby. The news you were pregnant came as a hell of a shock. I was lashing out, and feel really bad about the things I said. If you must know, I was half out of my mind with jealousy. But that was only part of it.'

'And the other part?' I prompted when it looked as if the silence was going to spread into infinity and Dad was going to come crashing back in any moment.

His voice was so low I had to strain to hear him. 'When Abbie died, I didn't just lose my wife. I lost my daughter as well. Abbie died giving birth. She'd been warned that it could be dangerous to have a baby, but she was determined. And in the end she wore me down and, much against my better judgement, and to the horror of her parents, I gave in. As I said, she was a very strong-willed woman, and far too used to having her own way. She was certain that she was right and all the medics were wrong.'

'I'm sorry,' I whispered. But I don't think he heard me.

'But, of course,' he went on, 'it was the other way round. And it was my fault, as her mother has pointed out to me many, many times since. If I'd been firmer with her — 'more of a man' was how my mother-in-law put it — I'd have persuaded her to consider adoption or give up on the idea of children altogether. Had I done so, she would still be alive. And I've been eaten up by that knowledge ever since.

Abbie died on the operating table, my daughter just three hours later. I buried them both on the same day. And I vowed I would never go through that again; I would never love anyone again, and I would certainly never father a child again. The pain of losing them was simply too great.'

My heart ached for him. 'I'm so sorry,' I whispered, though my words went unheeded.

'So there I was,' he went on, 'breaking rule number one by falling for you. Then, when you said you were pregnant . . . ' He shook his head. 'That wasn't jealousy. Well, OK, that too. But the overriding emotion was pure, one hundred per cent panic.'

'And now?' I reached across for his hand. 'What do you feel now?'

'About you? About the baby? Scared to death. Excited. And very, very much in love with you.'

He reached across the bed, one hand either side of me and, carefully avoiding the drip in my arm, bent forward and kissed me. Very softly, very slowly, our lips hardly touching, our breath intermingling. It was the sweetest, the gentlest of kisses, but full of the promise of all the other kisses to come and the knowledge that we had all the time in the world.

It was like the last piece of a jigsaw had just slotted into place. We heard a door open behind us, and my father's muttered 'Excuse me' before the door closed again.

* * *

That was just over eighteen months ago. Andrew didn't need a DNA test on Rory Benjamin Mulryan — one glance at my beautiful baby boy was enough to tell anyone who his father was, and I'll do my best to keep Ben's memory alive for him as he grows up.

Liam — a ridiculously doting uncle — is happy and settled in Poole, while Andrew has sold up and moved to the States with Jane to begin a new life together. But they say they'd like to stay in touch with Rory, and I'm happy about that. Andrew and Dad haven't exactly bonded over the cradle; but like I said to Maggie, happy endings only happen in her lovely books.

Except Dad and Maggie had their own happy ending, which is great, and Dad's now busy rebuilding *Storm Chaser*; they're planning to go off on an extended honeymoon sailing around the coastline of Britain when it's done. He's not selling the boatyard, as he's convinced Rory's going to have his grandfather's feeling for boats. But, I ask him, which grandfather?

Archie has a new love in his life now that Liam has left for good — he's transferred his devotion to Rory, whom he follows everywhere. So much so that when we move into our new home (old Sam's bungalow, a wedding present from Andrew, which Nick has been extending and renovating), Archie will be coming to live with us.

And me? Well, today is a very special day. It's the day Rory Benjamin Mulryan becomes Rory Benjamin Thorne and I become Mrs Caitlin Thorne. Nick and I are getting married in the village church where Ben is buried, and after the ceremony I intend to place my bouquet on his grave, as a thank-you to him for giving Nick and me our lovely and much-loved little boy.